The doctor suddenly stopped in his tracks, groaned and staggered backwards, holding his chest.

'Dr Harker?' said Tom.

Ocean grabbed hold of Dr Harker as he fell back and, as he did so, they saw an arrow sticking out from between his fingers.

● ●

'Fast-paced, brilliantly plotted, impeccably researched, the Tom Marlowe Adventures are historical fiction at its best' *Chris Riddell*

'The murder mystery provides a tightly woven plot while the early 18th-century background, with its public hangings, petty thieving and coffee houses, is lightly but vividly drawn' *Guardian*

'This is that rare beast – an intelligent, gripping thriller with an original plot, credible characters with strong relationships and a sense of time and place so vivid that you can virtually see, hear and taste 18th-century London' *Carousel*

'This is an exciting, atmospheric adventure which keeps you hooked to the end' *Primary Times*

'This will have readers, especially boys, sitting on the edge of their seats trying to keep just one step ahead of Tom' *Junior Education*

'An historical crime thriller – Cadfael for teens' *What's On in London*

D0307847

Also available by Chris Priestley:

THE WHITE RIDER
The second Tom Marlowe adventure

REDWULF'S CURSE
The third Tom Marlowe adventure

And for younger readers:

DOG MAGIC!
BILLY WIZARD

A Tom Marlowe Adventure

Death
and the
Arrow

C H R I S   P R I E S T L E Y

CORGI BOOKS

DEATH AND THE ARROW
A CORGI BOOK 9780552554756

First published in Great Britain by Doubleday,
an imprint of Random House Children's Books

Doubleday edition published 2003
Corgi Yearling edition published 2004
Corgi edition published 2006

3 5 7 9 10 8 6 4 2

The Random House Group Limited supports The Forest Stewardship
Council (FSC), the leading international forest certification organisation.
All our titles that are printed on Greenpeace approved FSC certified paper
carry the FSC logo. Our paper procurement policy can be found at:
www.rbooks.co.uk/environment.

Set in Sabon MT by
Falcon Oast Graphic Art Ltd.

Corgi Books are published by Random House Children's Books,
61–63 Uxbridge Road, London W5 5SA,
A Random House Group Company

Addresses for companies within The Random House Group Limited
can be found at: www.randomhouse.co.uk/offices.htm

THE RANDOM HOUSE GROUP Limited Reg. No. 954009
www.kidsatrandomhouse.co.uk

A CIP catalogue record for this book is available from the British Library.

Printed and bound in Great Britain by
CPI Cox & Wyman, Reading, RG1 8EX

For Sally

1

MURDER IN THE TOWN

It was an April morning in 1715. Ludgate Hill
was in full flow. Carriages and carts clattered
over the slippery cobbles and a thousand busy
feet pounded the pavements. It was barely noon
but the street was as dark as dusk, as chimney

after chimney puffed and spluttered like a sailor in a gin cellar.

A surgeon sniffed at the perfumed handle of his cane, trying to rid his nose of the mortuary stink, and cheered himself with the thought that there was a hanging tomorrow and he had been promised the corpse. An African, stolen by slavers from his native land, tried unsuccessfully to recall his people's word for sun. A red kite flew across the smoke-stained sky, trailing the bloody proceeds of a scavenging trip to Smithfield market. A soldier patted a sweep for luck. A wig-maker from Cheapside searched for his watch and finding his pocket empty shouted, '*Stop, thief!*' Gentlemen felt for their sword hilts, villains for their clasp knives. A constable cursed and ducked down an alleyway, but the pickpocket was long gone.

Hawkers of every kind called out, 'Oranges!' and 'Oysters!' and 'Won't you buy my . . .' this or that, until the air was filled with their deafening jabber and you could not tell who was selling milk and who was selling mousetraps.

And there, in the midst of all this, was Tom

Marlowe, fifteen years old, an apprentice at his father's printing shop under the sign of the Lamb and Lion in Fleet Street. Mr Marlowe printed all manner of things: posters and pamphlets, sermons and ballads – even the 'Last Dying Speeches' of the condemned.

Tom was taking a bundle of proofs of a scientific pamphlet to Dr Harker at his coffee house, The Quill, in St Paul's churchyard. The new cathedral towered above, its stonework still stark and soot-free, its great lead dome visible for miles around. Tom's father hated it. 'A dome?' he had said when it was finished. 'Are we Italians? No! A spire, Tom, a tower – that's England, boy.'

Tom, on the other hand, thought it the most amazing thing he had ever seen and never tired of looking at it.

Warm air swept over him as he opened the coffee-house door and a couple of the customers rustled their newspapers, irritated by the intrusion. Dr Harker was in his usual place over by the fire.

'Tom, lad,' he called and motioned with his cane for Tom to come and join him. 'A bowl of chocolate for my young friend! Sit yourself down, lad. How's your father, Tom?'

'He's well, thank you, Dr Harker.'

Dr Harker was Tom's favourite of all his father's customers and the doctor was, in his turn, very fond of the young apprentice. The doctor's own son was a navy man; he was away at sea most of the time and showed little interest in his father or his work when he was home. 'What is the point in knowing more than you *need* to know?' asked the son on his last visit. 'But I *need* to know *everything*!' answered the father. They were a puzzlement to each other.

But Tom could listen to the doctor all day long. He was so clever – 'stuffed full of learning', Mr Marlowe called him – and he had *done* so much. In his younger days he had sailed to the Americas and Africa and had dozens of cabinets chock-full of the curiosities he had found there. When he talked, he would wave his arms in the air, as if trying to catch the visions he was conjuring up for his young friend, and the curls of his periwig would shake, dusting his coat with powder.

It was magical for Tom. He had never done anything or been anywhere. His life, or so he felt, was as dull as the Fleet ditch and looking into Dr Harker's life was like looking into a sparkling jewel box.

'Another brandy,' said a voice to their right, 'to warm these old bones of mine.' It was the Reverend Purney, the chaplain of Newgate jail. He nodded over at Tom, took out his long clay pipe and flashed his yellow teeth; Purney was another of Mr Marlowe's clients.

'It would take a gallon of brandy to warm that hypocritical old buzzard,' whispered Dr Harker. 'Do you know what hypocritical means, Tom?'

'No, sir, I don't,' replied Tom.

'And long may it remain so,' said Dr Harker with a grin. 'Long may it remain so.'

At that moment a youth burst in with an armful of newspapers. 'Murder in the town!' he shouted – to no great effect, for murders were all too common in these violent times. '*Extraordinary* murder!' he called, perhaps a little disappointed at the response.

'How so?' called a wag by the window. 'Have

they caught the murderer then?' The coffee-house client-ele erupted into laughter.

'Beskewered by an arrow right through his heart, that's how so!' replied the youth. He had their attention now.

'An arrow?' said Dr Harker quietly to no one in particular. 'Now that is rather unusual.'

'It's the work of the Mohocks, I'll be bound!' said the Reverend Purney, and there was a grumbling of agreement. The newspapers had been full of horror stories about the gang of upper-class thugs.

'I think not,' said Dr Harker.

'Oh?' said Purney. 'And why not? They name themselves after savages and behave like savages. Murder with arrows would seem a logical step.'

'What difference does it make?' said a young man nearby. 'With lords for fathers and uncles in the government, they're never going to be chatting to you in the Condemned Hold, now are they, Reverend?'

Several people nodded and said, 'That's right,' but Dr Harker ignored this diversion.

'The Mohocks cannot be ruled out, I agree.

But we need more information. Do you have any other facts for us, lad?' he called to the youth.

'I do, sir! There's witnesses what say that this here skewered gent runs past them seconds before the deed, and on into a courtyard with no way out but locked doors – locked, mark you. They follows him and finds him nailed ... but not another soul in sight! Not a sparrow, not a tick.' A murmur ran round the room.

'But there's more,' said the youth, pointing his finger at no one in particular. 'It turns out that this here stiff was dead already.'

'Dead already?' said Dr Harker. 'What do you mean?'

'Well, sir,' replied the newspaper boy, smiling now that he had his audience in his grip, 'this here corpse – Leech was his name – he was a soldier-boy, fighting the French in the Americas, God save the King.'

'Yes, yes,' said Dr Harker impatiently. 'To the point, lad!'

'Well, it's like I was just saying. A military man, he was, and paid the price. Cut down by heathen savages. Murdered by Indians out in the

Americas while he was fighting the French some years ago!' Tom's eyes widened.

'What?' said Purney. 'Impossible!'

'Killed him dead, they did, and all the men with him.'

'Then there must be a mistake,' said the owner of the coffee house. 'The murdered man must be someone else.'

'No, sir. No mistake. His own mother lives not a spit away and verified him with her own teary eyes. His sergeant come down and did the same. There ain't no mistake.'

The customers began to mutter to themselves and mumble asides at their neighbours, but the newspaper boy held up his hand. 'And ask me how the Indians killed them. Go on, ask me.'

'Shot by arrows?' suggested Dr Harker.

'Arrows it was,' said the youth. The customers gasped and turned to the doctor in amazement.

'Come now,' he said with a shrug. 'It hardly took a genius to divine that if he had been killed by natives, they might use bows.' Even so, Tom noticed Dr Harker turned back to the newsboy with a contented smile. 'Is there more?' he asked.

'There is,' he was told. 'In his pocket they finds a card – a calling card, if you like. And you ain't never going to guess what was on it!'

There was a long pause – rather too long – and Dr Harker was forced to break the silence by saying, 'I rather fear that we won't. Could you do us the enormous favour of telling us?'

The coffee house filled with laughter again and the newspaper-seller blushed. 'In his pocket they finds a card,' he repeated, 'and on that card there's an embellishment – a figure of Death, no less, pointing one bony finger and looking like to chuck an arrow with the other hand. Now, gents, tell me if that ain't a story or what?'

Even the sour-faced Reverend Purney had to admit that it *was* quite a story – though one could not always believe what one heard or even what one read in the newspapers. He reminded the customers – again – that he had once heard a report of his own body being found floating in the Fleet. Everyone nodded and smiled, but several customers secretly hoped to see that report proved true.

2

FOG

By the time Tom left the coffee house, a thick sulphurous fog had taken hold of the city. It was the queasy colour of curdled milk and gripped his throat like a thief. He could see almost nothing in the murk and kept to the wall, dodging the other poor citizens as they coughed their way blindly towards him. He could hear the muffled clatter of horses' hooves and the *tick, tock* of walking sticks and boot heels; somewhere in the distance cattle were lowing as they made their way to market, and the smells of baking bread, fish, coffee and horse dung competed with the rotten-egg stink of the fog.

Tom had no fear of getting lost – he could make this journey blindfolded – but he kept up a brisk pace all the same, thinking all the while about arrows and Indians and murdered men. But most of all he thought about that hideous figure of Death, and shivered to his bones.

In this state of mind, Tom could be forgiven for letting out a shriek when a hand reached out from a doorway and almost pulled him off his feet. There was a peal of rough laughter and then a cough like nails shaken in a rusty pot. It was Will.

Whenever Tom went out on business these days, his father shouted, 'And mind who you're talking to, lad!' And though no one was mentioned by name, they both knew that it was Will who Tom's father had in mind.

Mr Marlowe thoroughly disapproved of Will and would fly into a rage at the mere mention of his name. He could not understand what a lad like Tom could possibly want with the company of such a rogue as Will. And rogue he certainly was.

'Why can't you just say hello like everyone else?' said Tom, smiling now.

'What's with the screaming, Tom? I thought for a minute I'd grabbed a Frenchman by mistake!' Will wheezed and spat on the ground.

'Very funny, Will, very funny. I wonder you don't get yourself a booth at Bartholomew Fair and make yourself some honest money, you being such a clown and all,' said Tom, giving Will a shove in the arm.

'Now, now – no need for that. But you won't rile me, Tom, for I've had a good day.'

'Give it back,' said Tom with a sigh.

'What?' pleaded Will. 'I ain't done nothing.'

'The watch, Will. Hand it over.'

'I don't believe it! There's no way you could've felt it. How come you knew, Tom? How? I'm a master, I am. I could take the ring from a bull's nose, with him none the wiser. I just can't see how you could've felt that – I just can't . . .'

Will muttered away to himself and kicked out at the wall. Tom had felt nothing – Will was every bit the master of his art he claimed to be, but he had taken to picking Tom's pocket every time they met and Tom now merely guessed and heartily enjoyed the effect it had on his friend.

Will handed back the pocket watch. A grin suddenly shone out from his grimy face. 'Come on.' And so the two of them walked on together through the fog, each, as usual, fascinated by the other's very different life; Tom recalling, yet again, the part his pocket watch had played in their first meeting . . .

Their friendship had begun one August a couple of years before, at Bartholomew Fair in Smithfield. Tom loved the fair. There was just so much to see: jugglers and fire-eaters, tightrope walkers and conjurors; there were gypsies too, like parrots come to rest among sparrows, with their gold earrings and rainbow clothes.

Tom had been standing at the edge of the fair

listening to a strange character dressed in sack-cloth preaching about the end of the world, when he heard a commotion behind. He had turned just in time to see a driverless horse and carriage rushing towards him.

He had not even had time to call out before he was knocked off his feet; he hit the pavement with a winding thud. But he had not been mown down by the horse or the carriage; he had been pushed out of their path and into a side alley.

Tom looked up at the dirty face of his saviour. 'Y-you saved my life,' he stammered.

'You know, I reckon you might be right at that,' said the lad with a grin. They got to their feet and dusted themselves down.

Tom held out his hand and smiled. 'Tom Marlowe,' he said.

'The name's William Piggot,' said Will with a grin, 'but most people call me—'

'A thieving little cockroach,' said a voice behind them.

They turned to see a tall man dressed in black looming over them, a billowing powdered wig under his tricorn hat, one hand on the hilt of his silver sword. Behind him were two other men, also dressed in black.

'Mr Hitchin, sir . . .' began Will, his face a little paler under the grime.

'That's Under-marshal Hitchin to you, scum,' said the tall man. 'Make sure we are not disturbed.' This was directed at his companions, who retreated to block the entrance to the alley.

Hitchin's sneer suddenly became a crocodile grin as he turned to Tom. 'And who is this fine fellow?'

'Tom Marlowe,' said Tom a little nervously. 'Of the Lamb and Lion printing house.'

'And what is a respectable lad like you doing keeping company with one of London's most notorious divers?' Tom turned to Will, who cocked his head and shrugged. 'I see that young Piggot has failed to mention his pickpocketing skills. Tut, tut, Will. Don't be shy, now.'

'Tom, I—' began Will, but Hitchin hit him hard across the side of the head with the back of his hand. Will staggered two steps back, shaking his head, but made no protest.

'Now then,' said Hitchin, pushing Tom gently

to one side. 'If I could just ask you to stand back, Master Marlowe, we shall see what our filthy little friend has in his pockets.' He slowly put on a pair of calfskin gloves and stepped over to Will, smiling. Suddenly he grabbed the boy by the throat with one hand and began patting his clothes with the other. 'Now, what have we here?' he said, and pulled out a silver pocket watch and chain. He squinted at it, reading an inscription on the back: '"For my son, Tom". Well, that's strange, is it not? Your name is Will—'

'The watch is mine,' said Tom.

'Well, that explains it,' said Hitchin.

'I've never seen that watch in my life!' exclaimed Will.

Hitchin hit him again. Harder this time. 'Tell it to someone that cares,' he growled. 'Tell it to the hangman, for all I care!'

'I gave him the watch,' said Tom suddenly.

Hitchin and Will looked equally surprised. 'You did what?' said Hitchin.

'I gave him the watch,' said Tom. 'He saved my life just now. There must be people who saw. I gave him my watch as a reward.'

Hitchin walked slowly towards Tom and leaned forward until the tip of his nose was touching the tip of Tom's. 'And you would swear this in a court of law?'

'I would,' said Tom, edging back a little.

Hitchin remained frozen for a few seconds, staring into Tom's eyes as if looking for something hidden there. Then he suddenly stood upright, took off his gloves and smiled. 'Very well, then, Master Marlowe,' he said. 'I will bid you good day.' And with that he walked away, his two men falling into step behind him.

'That was quick thinking, Tom,' said Will with a laugh. 'I thought he was—'

Tom punched Will on the jaw and sent him spinning towards the wall.

'What's this?' said Will, rubbing his jaw. 'Do I look like I enjoy being smacked?'

'You stole my watch, you thief,' said Tom, fists clenched.

'Thief I am,' said Will, 'but I never stole your watch, you muffin. And don't think about giving me an-other tap or I shall have to black your eye.'

'I suppose it just hopped into your pocket on its own, did it?' shouted Tom.

'It didn't have to,' said Will. 'It had Hitchin to give it a leg-up, didn't it?'

'What are you talking about? How could Hitchin—?'

'Think about it,' said Will. 'When Hitchin eased you out the way, that's when he made the dive. He's not bad, neither. I felt him make the drop into my pocket, but then it's bread and butter to me. I've had more practice.' He put a hand to his chest. 'Look, I swear on my mother's grave. I didn't take your watch, Tom.'

'But why?' said Tom, fists still clenched. 'Why would Hitchin try to get you hanged?'

'Because he's a villain, Tom. They call him a thief-taker, but he's a bigger crook than any he brings in. He has half the pickpockets in London on a leash. He gets them to rob such and such a gent and then charges the selfsame toff a finder's fee for returning the goods. He's been trying to get me to work for him for ages. He's just letting me know he can get me dangled any time he likes. But I'm my own man.'

Tom stared at him and then looked away towards the end of the alley. His hands relaxed.

'I swear, Tom,' said Will. 'I never took your watch. I ain't no liar.' Will smiled a crooked smile. 'Well, not at this particular moment anyways.'

Tom laughed. Will held out his hand and Tom shook it.

'Come on,' said Will. 'Let's get out of this stinking alley.'

'I suppose your mother is dead?' said Tom, remembering Will's oath.

'As a hangman's heart,' replied Will.

'Mine too,' said Tom.

Will stopped and slapped Tom in the chest with the back of his hand. 'Then ain't we like brothers in a way?'

'Yes,' said Tom. 'I suppose we are.'

And so, in a way, they had been since that day.

They were an odd couple, but well matched in many ways. Each had a ready wit and a quick temper and both, as young boys, had lost their mothers, which left them with a sadness and an unspoken yearning for something more than they had.

Physically they were very different, though, with Tom black-haired and stocky, and Will blond and skinny as a whippet. Will's clothes were shabby and often much too big for him, emphasizing his slight frame. And he was always in need of a wash that never seemed to come.

Tom talked about his father and the printing shop and Dr Harker. Will loved to hear of the doctor's travels, for just like Tom he had yet to travel five miles from the house in which he was born. For his part Will gave a watered-down account of his life as a member of London's army of pickpockets and petty thieves.

'As it happens,' said Will, suddenly remembering their earlier conversation, 'I don't need your poxy watch, Tom, for I have a rather splendid one of my own. Now let me see – what is the time?' With a theatrical flourish, he produced a beautiful gold watch and chain – the very same watch the Cheapside wig-maker had searched for in vain earlier that day.

'Will! For God's sake! Put it away!'

'All right, calm down, Tom,' Will replied, hiding the watch inside his coat. 'Don't have a seizure! There's no one to see us in this fog. Don't get so flustered.'

'*Don't get so flustered?* You could swing for that – and me along with you for not speaking up!'

'No one's going to swing, Tom, though it's good to hear you won't be peaching on me . . .'

'It's not funny, Will. You'll be picking the hangman's pocket one day.'

'Well, you're in a cheery mood today,' said Will, a little crossly. 'You know what I am – what I does. Don't come the parson with me, Tom.'

They both looked down at the ground in front of them and waited for the other to speak. As usual in these situations, it was Will who broke the silence.

'Well, as it happens, Master Marlowe, I happen to have gone and got meself a job.'

'*You?*' gasped Tom.

'Yes, me, you cheeky rogue,' said Will, sounding a little hurt.

'Sorry, Will. That's great news, really it is. I was just a little, well, *surprised*, is all.'

'Yeah, well. I got feelings too, Tom. Lots of 'em.'

'I know, Will, honest I do. Tell me about it. What is the work exactly?'

'Well,' said Will, puffing himself up a little, 'I happen to be in the employ of a certain gent I know who has paid me to perform certain very delicate duties.'

'Hmm,' said Tom, raising an eyebrow. 'It is *honest* work, isn't it, Will?'

Will grinned broadly and slapped Tom on the chest with the back of his hand. 'Listen to you. You are such a worrier, Tom. But I can't talk about it, not even to you. Sworn to secrecy and all that.'

'Will . . .'

'I've got to go, Tom. We'll talk later.' And with that Will set off towards the City.

'Will!' called Tom. 'Is it *honest*?'

Will had all but melted into the fog and was a vague and pale sketch when he turned to call back to Tom. 'You could say it's the *opposite* of what I normally do!' Then he turned and, with a little hacking laugh, disappeared like a ghost at dawn.

Tom was just trying to make some kind of sense of what Will had said when a breeze blew in from the Thames and cleared a patch of fog, allowing the houses on the other side of the street to come briefly into view.

Within an instant the fog had closed back in, but in that instant Tom could have sworn he saw someone running along the roof ridge of one of the buildings. He waited to see if the fog would shift again but it seemed set. Tom shook his head. Maybe he was starting to imagine things.

3

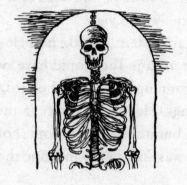

SURGEONS' HALL

A few days later Tom's father gave him a parcel to deliver to Dr Harker. As Tom was leaving, his father called out to him, without looking up from his work, 'And I'd be obliged if you went straight there and came straight back.'

'Father?' said Tom.

'You were seen, Tom. Talking to that – that article.' Mr Marlowe banged his fist on a pile of paper, sending the top five sheets to the floor. 'Why must you go against me, Tom? What is a fine lad like you doing with someone of that sort?'

Tom could think of nothing to say that he had not said before and so he remained silent, knowing that nothing angered his father more.

'Blast it, Tom! I'm glad your mother's not alive to see what company you keep!' Mr Marlowe regretted the words as soon as they left his mouth, but it was too late. Tom stood for a moment, frozen by the force of rage and hurt, and then turned and made for the street.

Tom walked briskly, his eyes stinging with unshed tears, until he reached Dr Harker's house, which was in a small courtyard off Fleet Street. He climbed the three stone steps up to the deep-green door and rapped the brass knocker. A maidservant let him in and showed him into the study.

'Ah, Tom!' said Dr Harker, looking up from a

huge leather-bound book. 'Good to see you! Come and sit yourself down. May I?' Tom handed him the parcel of printed pamphlets.

Dr Harker picked up the Arabian dagger he always used to open parcels, cut through the string and, as usual, jabbed his thumb. 'Bother and beeswax!' He searched for a hand-kerchief and knocked a candlestick to the floor. 'Oh, never mind, never mind,' he said, sucking his thumb and eagerly tearing off the wrapping paper with his other hand. 'Excellent! Wonderful! Your father is an artist, Tom, a veritable Michelangelo.'

Tom smiled half-heartedly. Dr Harker could see that something was wrong, but knew his young friend well enough not to approach the matter head on. If Tom wanted to talk, he would. If not, the Inquisition and all their racks and thumbscrews would not have been able to make him. 'Tell me,' said the doctor, pointing to the pamphlet, 'have you read it?'

'Of course, Doctor,' said Tom. He always read Dr Harker's pamphlets.

'And what do you think?'

'Well, I don't claim to understand it all, but there's going to be an eclipse, isn't there?' said Tom, brightening now, eager for the distraction.

'There is indeed. A solar eclipse. And if the sky clears for long enough, we'll see it. Right here in London, Tom – imagine it: the shadow of the moon passing over the city.'

Tom tried to imagine it but could not. He had looked at the diagram on Dr Harker's pamphlet but he could not see how night and day could be so weirdly intermingled. It seemed impossible.

'It will be an unforgettable event, Tom. If the weather is kind to us, it will be stupendous.'

'They say it's an evil omen, don't they, Dr Harker? The eclipse, I mean,' said Tom.

'Nonsense, lad! Utter nonsense! There is nothing *super*natural here, Tom. It is all absolutely *natural*. Is the swinging of a pendulum an evil omen . . . or the movement of the hands on a clock face? All we are seeing is the workings of the universe, the movements of its marvellous machine!

'Sometimes I despair of this great city of ours, Tom. England is home to men of incomparable reasoning, lad. Men like Halley and Wren – not to mention Newton, of course. Giants among men, Tom; giants among men.' Dr Harker's face was beginning to flush and his arms, as always, began to wave wildly, the more excited he became.

'And yet,' he cried, banging the flat of his hand down on the desk and making a pot of ink jump half an inch in the air. 'And yet, we are also home to a coven of the most scandalously dishonest charlatans and rogues imaginable. One cannot walk the streets of this town without tripping over astrologers and diviners, so-called wise women and cunning men. Conning men, more like!' Again he banged the table; again the inkpot jumped.

'If a gentleman has his sword stolen, what does he do? He pays some crafty cunning man to try and divine, by magic, where his property is gone to and who may have taken it. By magic! Is this the eighteenth century or the fourteenth?'

'The eighteenth,' said Tom helpfully.

Dr Harker smiled, feeling a little foolish at his

outburst. He was also hot under his periwig and he eased it off, putting it carefully on its mahogany stand. Then he scratched the bristles on his shaven head and put on his crimson silk turban.

'But what choice does the gentleman have in any event, Tom? To go to the likes of that scoundrel and so-called thief-taker, Hitchin.' Dr Harker looked across at Tom and smiled. 'Of course, you and he have met, have you not? How is young Will Piggot?'

'He's well enough, thank you, Doctor,' said Tom. 'Though my father would see him transported if it were up to him.'

'Come now, Tom. Your father only has your interests at heart. Will leads a dangerous life. Your father does not want you touched by that danger, that is all.'

'But I want something more than ink and paper,' said Tom. 'You can understand that, can't you, sir?'

Dr Harker nodded. 'I can, Tom,' he said. 'You want adventure, lad. I was just the same at your age. But I understand your father too. You know that he loves you dearly, don't you, lad?'

Tom looked away. The two of them sat in silence a while until the doctor spoke again. 'Have I ever told you about my voyage to Constantinople, Tom?' He had, but Tom was more than happy to hear it again and in no time Dr Harker was off.

As always, the doctor leaped from one subject to another, happy to talk while he had such an attentive listener. One moment he was telling Tom about the minarets of Constantinople, the next he was showing him rock from the slopes of some far-off volcano, then a pair of shoes from the Americas, made of hide and decorated with tiny beads. Every now and then he would stretch across to pull down a book from his vast library, pointing to pictures of places Tom could only dream about.

Suddenly, Dr Harker broke off from what he was saying and looked at his pocket watch. 'What am I thinking of? Come, Tom. We'll be late if we don't hurry.'

'Late?' said Tom, chasing after the doctor. 'Late for what?'

'For our appointment, of course! You've heard there's been another murder?'

'Yes, of course,' said Tom. He had heard the newspaper-sellers calling out the news as he walked from the print shop. 'Another Death and the Arrow murder . . .'

'Exactly!' said Dr Harker. 'And that's why I've arranged this little meeting.'

'What meeting?' said Tom, struggling to keep up with the doctor, who had already put his wig back on and was descending the stairs.

'With Dr Cornelius,' he said, opening the front door and marching out into the street.

'Who is Dr Cornelius, sir?' asked Tom.

'Probably the finest surgeon in the land.'

Tom stopped in his tracks. 'A s-s-surgeon?' he stammered.

Dr Harker laughed. 'Come now, Tom. Surely a clever lad like you isn't frightened of a medical man?'

'I didn't say I was frightened,' said Tom defensively. 'I just don't like them, that's all.' He shared the popular revulsion for 'anatomizers' and their habits. Dr Harker laughed again.

'They're vultures,' Tom went on. 'They rob graves – or at least they pay others to do it for them. They steal corpses and cut them up. And people pay to watch. It's ... it's ...' He shuddered, lost for words.

'I don't approve of theft, of course,' said the doctor, 'but how else can they learn about the living? We need to look at the inner workings of the body.' Tom shuddered again. 'The work they do now will one day save lives, Tom, I'm sure of it. You must keep an open mind on these things.'

But Tom was not convinced. He wanted to be a man of reason like the doctor, but there was something about the idea of men cutting up the bodies of other men that made him shiver. It was an instinctive, animal dread.

Dr Harker smiled at Tom's discomfort and gave up trying to convince him. They walked on in silence through Ludgate and turned onto Old Bailey. They could hear a trial going on in the courtyard outside the Sessions House. The crowd let out a groan, and a woman screamed, 'No!'

'Another poor soul has been sent to the

gallows, by the sound of it,' said Dr Harker. 'Ah, here we are: Surgeons' Hall.'

Tom was just thinking how convenient it was that the Surgeons' Hall was so close to the court, when he was taken aback to see what looked for all the world like a magpie in human form.

'And there's the very man we've come to see,' said Dr Harker.

A little way off, with his back towards them, stood a tall, thin man all in black; black, that is, apart from the powdered periwig that tumbled down over his shoulders and the skinny, white-stockinged legs showing between his breeches and his shiny black shoes. His pointed black tricorn hat gave the strangest illusion of a huge crow's beak.

'Dr Cornelius!' shouted Dr Harker.

The man turned to look at them. His face was pale and gaunt, his piercing eyes so deep set that the brows cast a deep shadow over them. Tom thought him the most sinister-looking person he had ever seen. If he had not been at Dr Harker's side, he would have spun on his heels and run.

33

'Josiah,' said Dr Cornelius. 'A pleasure to see you, as always.'

'And you, Jonathan,' said Dr Harker.

The two men shook hands warmly and enquired after each other's work and health. Tom stood nearby, feeling a little self-conscious.

'Ah, Jonathan,' said Dr Harker. 'Come and meet my very good friend, Tom Marlowe. His father owns the Lamb and Lion print shop.'

'Delighted to make your acquaintance, Master Marlowe.' Tom shook the gloved hand that was held out to him and smiled reluctantly. Dr Cornelius raised an eyebrow and grinned. 'You do not have a high opinion of surgeons, I fear, Master Marlowe,' he said.

'I don't mean to give offence,' said Tom.

Dr Cornelius grinned again. 'But all the same, I see you do not deny it.'

'Well,' said Dr Harker, interrupting diplomatically, 'what have you got to show us, Jonathan?'

'Follow me, gentlemen,' said Dr Cornelius.

He led them through the building to a set of huge double doors. These opened into a large room, lit by a skylight in the high ceiling. At one side of the room were wooden seats in curved rows and skeletons hung in niches set into the walls. Directly below the skylight was a large table, and on the table, under a stained white cloth, was a corpse.

Dr Cornelius raised the perforated grip of his cane to his nose and sniffed at the perfume within. The air was heavy with the smell of decay. A fly settled on Tom's hand and he brushed it away with a shudder. He could not take his eyes from the corpse on the table.

'I gather you saw the first victim of the Death and the Arrow murders, Jonathan?' said Dr Harker.

'That I did, Josiah,' replied Dr Cornelius. 'Until his mother claimed the body, that is. It was a fascinating case. You know the story?'

'That he had supposedly already been killed by an arrow in the Americas?' said Dr Harker. 'Yes, it's intriguing, is it not? Do you have anything to add to the story, Jonathan?'

'Well, not very much, I'm afraid. There was one interesting thing though. The shaft of the arrow had been snapped off before the body came to me, but it was still clear from which direction the arrow had come. A very strange business . . .'

'I don't understand,' said Dr Harker.

'The arrow came from above,' said Dr Cornelius, pointing upwards.

'Extraordinary!' exclaimed Dr Harker.

'I have the second victim here, if you'd like to see,' said Dr Cornelius.

'Could I? I'd be fascinated.'

'Our man was almost killed some time ago. He carries a old wound on his back, below his right shoulder. I cannot be sure, of course, but I would hazard a guess that it was made by a musket ball.'

'A musket ball?' said Dr Harker. 'Then perhaps he was a soldier, like the first victim. This is very interesting.'

Tom felt a bead of sweat trickle down his face. He was having to concentrate to keep the doctors in focus as they pulled back the sheet.

'Some fool has pulled the arrow out of this one, as you can see,' said Dr Cornelius. 'Look at the mess they've made. But it would be my guess that once again the arrow was fired from above . . .'

Tom fell to the floor.

Tom came to sitting on the steps outside Surgeons' Hall.

'You fainted, lad,' said Dr Harker. Tom felt well enough to blush. 'Good to see some colour back in those cheeks,' the doctor continued with a smile. 'Can you stand?'

'I think so,' said Tom, rising shakily. 'Did Dr Cornelius tell you anything interesting?'

'Yes, lad. Indeed he did.'

Tom waited for Dr Harker to continue, but he simply began to walk off in the direction of Fleet Street. 'What did he tell you, Doctor?' asked Tom, trotting after him.

'Many things, lad. For one thing, someone broke the arrow that shot our first victim and took away the flight. Odd, don't you think?'

The whole business seemed odd to Tom, and no part odder than the next, but he said, 'Yes, Doctor, very odd,' all the same.

'And by the way,' said Dr Harker, rooting around in his coat pocket, 'the second of the men had this on him.' He held up a card in front of Tom's startled face. The Death and the Arrow card.

4

NEWGATE

The following day Tom was on yet another errand for his father, but he had none of the spring that marked his stride when he was paying a visit to Dr Harker; this was a chore he always dreaded. Today he was delivering to the

Reverend Purney in Newgate prison.

Tom walked past the waxworks, crossed the Fleet and made his way up Old Bailey, only just managing to jump out of the path of an on-coming sedan chair. Chairmen stop for no one – they shout, and those not nimble enough to move are clattered like skittles.

The sun leaked through a filthy blanket of clouds, sending beams of light across the city. A balladeer strummed tunelessly at a broken lute, but when he sang his voice was as clear and sweet as spring water:

'When first I came to London Town,
My fortune for to find . . .'

The song was interrupted by the arrival of half a dozen sheep and a pursuing shepherd boy. The sheep had been heading for Smithfield but had bolted from their flock and were making a bid for freedom down Old Bailey. The balladeer was knocked off his feet, much to the amusement of passers-by, and Tom did not quite succeed in hiding his own laughter. The balladeer shot him an angry glance and Tom continued guiltily on his way.

A sunbeam struck Newgate as he reached the top of Old Bailey. It was actually one of the gates to the City of London; the prison was built into rooms above its arches and in buildings on either side. Will and his kind called it the Whit, because it had been built with Lord Mayor Dick Whittington's money centuries before. The stench from it made the rest of the city smell sweet in comparison.

Newgate was a fearful place and Tom could not help but think of Will whenever he came here. Pickpockets and highwaymen waited to have their fates decided at the Sessions House nearby; waited to be branded, flogged or put in the stocks; to be transported as slave labour for stealing a silk handkerchief or a wig; to be hanged.

'Hello, sweetheart!' shrieked a voice above him. It came from one of the iron-grilled windows of the Women's Hold above the arch-way. 'Give us a smile, then!' He smiled weakly at the two women who pressed their filthy faces against the rusty bars. 'Buy us a drink, pretty boy!' Tom blushed.

'She-Devils!' muttered a voice behind him. It was Purney. The women saw him and a great squawking erupted from the third floor; all of a sudden a hand shot out and emptied a chamber pot. Tom and the reverend only just managed to get out of the way in time as they both dived into the cover of the arch, the contents of the chamber pot splashing on the cobbles behind them. They could hear crazed laughter above.

'Why we don't just hang the lot of them I will not understand. Instead of which we ship them off to the Americas and after seven short years they're back again. It's a disgrace! No, hang them all. It's for God to be merciful, not us!'

Tom said nothing, but only because he had promised his father that he would not argue with the Reverend Purney. 'I know he's an old goat, Tom, but we need all the business we can get,' Mr Marlowe would say. But Tom wished the women had hit their mark all the same.

He and the reverend usually conducted their business in The Quill, but Purney was busy that day, trying to wheedle a little more information out of the men in the Condemned Hold. It was a perk of his job that he could sell copies of their 'confessions' on hanging days. It was these 'accounts' that Tom's father printed. 'A pretty trade for a man of God,' Dr Harker called it.

A steady flow of visitors filed past them to pay to see their friends and relatives – and accomplices: a young woman sobbing pitifully into a lace handkerchief, a tall man with a dead eye, a stout gent in a powdered periwig, a pockmarked butcher's boy in a bloodstained apron.

'Here are your copies, Reverend Purney,' said Tom, eager to get the matter over with.

'Yes, yes,' said Purney, peeling back a little of the wrapping paper with a grin. 'That all seems to be in order; my thanks to your father. Let me get your money, Master Marlowe . . .' He made a great show of bringing out the bag of money in payment for the printing. Given the nature of many of the visitors to Newgate, this was downright dangerous, and Tom could not rid himself of the idea that the old devil did it on purpose.

Intentional or not, Tom lost no time in

quitting Purney's company and set off towards Ludgate Hill, throwing anxious glances over his shoulder as he did so. But no one followed him and gradually he breathed more freely and slowed his pace, smiling at his own nervousness. 'Blast that old crow Purney,' he muttered to himself.

Suddenly a hand shot out from an alleyway and dragged him sideways from the street. He tried to call out but the hand clamped across his mouth and a voice close by him hissed, 'Hush, Tom!' It was Will.

'I wish you'd stop doing that!' whispered Tom when his friend took his hand away. 'Where have you been, anyway?'

But Will was barely listening. He was shooting fevered glances this way and that, like a bird that fears the cat's pounce. When he looked back at Tom his eyes were wild. 'I'm a dead man, Tom. As sure as if I was in my shroud,' he hissed.

'Will?' said Tom. 'What's happened? Is it Hitchin?'

'Ain't got time to tell, Tom. But I'm dead, you have my word on it.'

'But, Will—' started Tom, but Will cut him off and handed him a leather purse, fat with coins.

'See me buried proper, Tom. I ain't got no one else,' he whispered, a tear tumbling down his cheek.

'No!' said Tom. 'There must be something we can do, whatever the trouble is—'

'There ain't nothing!' spat Will. 'You got to swear to me, Tom, for friendship's sake. A coffin. I don't want those anatomizers carving me up like a goose.' He was sobbing now. 'Swear it, Tom, I'm begging you!'

'I swear, Will,' said Tom, crying himself now.

'That's settled then,' said Will, suddenly calm. 'And now I must bid you good day, Master Marlowe . . .'

'No, Will. Let's go to my father . . . or to Dr Harker—'

Will suddenly lunged at Tom and grabbed him by his collar, staring into his face. 'No one can help me, Tom! No one!' He held up a card in front of Tom's face. Grimy and dog-eared though it was, it still clearly showed a figure of Death holding an arrow.

Tom gasped. 'Will! Where did you get that? Those murders, Will . . .'

'Don't say you have me down as a murderer now, Tom?' said Will with a weak smile. 'No, I ain't killed no one and it ain't Jack Ketch's noose I'm feared of, neither.'

'Then what . . .?'

'Don't ask, Tom. No good could come of you knowing any more, I swear . . .' Once again Will became calm and grabbed Tom in a tight bear hug. 'Remember me,' he whispered and turned to walk away. Tom tried to stop him but Will shrugged him off. 'Promise you'll see me buried right, Tom, and then let me go. I wouldn't want you hurt for all the world, and death is catching . . .'

With that he bolted away as only he could, vanishing into the city he knew so well, leaving Tom standing forlornly in the alleyway, his face wet with Will's tears and his own.

5

ANOTHER STRANGE MURDER

It was dark by the time Tom reached Dr Harker's house and the lamps were lit. He could think of nowhere else to turn and he hammered wildly on the door with his fist. 'Dr Harker!' he yelled. 'Dr Harker!'

An angry maid opened the door and told him crossly that her master was not at home.

'Where is he? I have to find him!'

'Be off with you,' she said. 'And come back tomorrow when the doctor is at home.'

'You know me!' shouted Tom. 'I've been here many times. I need to see the doctor now!'

Something in the desperate way he said it softened the maid's heart a little. 'He's at the coffee house,' she said after a moment's pause. 'Now on your way, or I shall fetch a constable!'

But Tom was already running. A toothless old watchman shouted out to him to stop, but Tom ran on regardless through a fine drizzle that polished the cobbled streets.

He knew that something must be terribly wrong for Will to talk that way. He just wasn't the sort to say a thing like that without good cause. Tom ran as if in a kind of trance, unable to think of anything but an overriding need to help his friend.

He could not ask his father for help – he could not even *tell* his father – but he was sure that Dr Harker would come to his aid, that Dr Harker would know what to do. He said this to himself as he ran, in time with his feet on the pavement. 'The doctor will know what to do, the doctor will know what to do . . .'

Tom almost fell into the coffee shop, gasping for breath. When he looked over to the fire, he saw Dr Harker in his usual place. Sitting next to him was Mr Marlowe.

'Tom, lad,' said his father. 'What are you doing here at this time?'

'I . . . I . . .' stammered Tom, looking back and forth between the two men. He almost ran out again.

'Come on, sit yourself down and spit it out,' laughed his father. 'What's troubling you?'

Tom sat down and stared down into his lap, fighting back tears.

'Tom?' said Dr Harker, seeing there really was something very wrong.

Tom hung his head and began to sob. 'It's Will . . .' he began, choking as he spoke.

'*Will?*' shouted his father.

'Mr Marlowe, I thought we had agreed that—' interrupted Dr Harker, but Tom's father put his hand up to stop him. He lowered his voice and turned back to Tom.

'Have I not strictly forbidden you to talk to that – that filthy little jackdaw?' he asked solemnly. 'Must you go against me at every turn?'

'But, Father . . .'

'Have I not *strictly forbidden it*?' he asked again.

'Yes, but . . .' Tom began again.

'Give me the watch, Tom,' said his father quietly, holding out his hand.

Tom looked at his father, then at Dr Harker, then back to his father once more. 'But . . .'

'*Give me that watch!*' his father yelled, banging his fist on the table and attracting the attention of everyone in the room.

'Mr Marlowe, *please*!' said Dr Harker.

Tom's father nodded, raised his hand briefly in apology and continued in a lower voice once more. 'I gave you that watch as a sign of how I've come to depend on you, son. To show how much I trust you and—'

'Please don't,' said Tom. 'I'm sorry I went

against you, Father, but Will's my friend. And he's in trouble.'

'Friend? Trouble? *Trouble?* Of course the little rogue's in trouble. He'll be in trouble till the day he chokes at Tyburn!'

'Don't say that!' shouted Tom, getting to his feet. His eyes were wild and his fists were clenched.

'You dare shout at me?' said Tom's father in amazement. 'You *dare* . . .?'

'Gentlemen, please . . .' said Dr Harker, making calming gestures with his hands.

'You dare shout at me?' repeated his father, standing up himself. 'Are these the manners your so-called friend has taught you? You dare to go against me? To take that wretch's side against your own kin!'

'I'd rather count Will a friend than all the Purneys in this world.'

'What the raging inferno has Purney got to do with anything?' shouted his father. 'Purney can go to hell for all I care, and I dare say shall . . .' He suddenly realized what he was saying and turned to see several customers nodding with approval. 'Purney's no friend of mine!' he said finally, turning back to Tom.

'But Will is a friend of mine. And I'll not desert him!' shouted Tom.

Tom's father, his face turning gradually purple, opened his mouth to speak but was cut short by the crash of the coffee-shop door as the newsboy rushed in.

'Murder!' he shouted. 'Another strange murder in the town!' All eyes in the coffee house turned from Tom and his father to the newsboy.

'Was it arrows again?' shouted Dr Harker, keen to make the most of the interruption and calm the tempers of his two friends.

'No, sir; strangled.' A murmur went round the room.

'Then why "strange"?'

'Well, sir,' said the youth, 'now I'm glad you asked. I says "strange" 'cos although he didn't have the arrows, he did have the card.'

'Explain yourself, lad,' said the doctor, but before the youth could speak Tom yelled, 'Who was it that was killed? Who was it that was killed?' The cry was so sudden and so passionate that it silenced the room. Dr Harker and Tom's father stared at him.

'What is it, Tom?' said the doctor.

'Who was it that was killed?' repeated Tom, quietly now, tears in his eyes.

'There ain't no need for shouting,' said the newsboy. 'I ain't no—'

'Just tell the lad, for goodness' sake!' said Dr Harker.

'All right, all right. As you're so interested, like; his name was Pigeon, Padget ... no, no, wait, Piggot. Yeah, that's it – William Piggot.'

Tom stared ahead like a madman. He shook his head and mouthed the word, 'No,' soundlessly. A great black wave seemed to crash over him and he thought he might fall over. His father rose to his feet and started towards him, but Tom spun round and stopped him in his tracks with the violence in his face. He took out the watch and tossed it across the room towards him. 'There,' he said coldly. 'Keep it. I never did deserve it.'

'Tom,' began his father again.

'He – was – my – *friend*!'

'Tom!' called his father, but Tom was already out of the door and running for all he was worth through the dark and twisting lanes, screaming out in a bitter rage of sadness until his heart was fit to burst or break.

6

A FUNERAL IN THE RAIN

London hardly noticed the passing of a boy like Will. The great city lumbered on its busy way, untroubled by the loss of yet another of its poor children, closing up over the gap he had left. Soon it would be as though he had never existed.

Or so things might have been, had it not been for Tom Marlowe. Whatever his father might think – and he and his father had barely spoken since their argument in the coffee house – Tom felt a bond with Will that even death could not break. He was true to his word, and with Dr Harker's help he used the money Will had given him to buy a coffin; Will would not be surgeons' meat.

On a day of constant and fitting drizzle Will's young body was laid to rest in the churchyard of St Bride's in Fleet Street. As the church bells chimed, a flock of jackdaws burst from the steeple, calling out and flying off towards the river, and a seagull cried forlornly from a nearby chimney top. The church spire jabbed the sky.

The only face in the graveyard that was not downcast belonged to the sexton, who leaned against the wall at a respectful distance, puffing on a clay pipe, leaning on a shovel, waiting to fill in the hole he had dug the day before. One grave was much like another to him.

The rain blackened the headstones and soaked

into the heap of clay beside the grave; it mingled with the tears of the mourners as they said their goodbyes to Will and turned away. Tom found it hard to leave the graveside but let himself be led away by Dr Harker. The sexton tapped out his pipe and picked up his shovel.

Will Piggot had been a popular character and the churchyard was full of the most extraordinary-looking people – molls, rogues and cutpurses – but Dr Harker greeted them all with the same civility as if they had been Justices of the Peace. He took control of the proceedings as Will's father might have done, had he not drunk himself to death five years before, and it was greatly appreciated by all who came – particularly Tom, who could never have managed without him. But everyone knew Tom's part in the proceedings.

'He's a good lad though, ain't he, bless him, seeing our Will done right?' said a pale, skinny, pockmarked girl as she patted Tom on the shoulder. 'And him from a decent home and everything.'

'That he is, Bess. You done him proud, boy – and yourself.' There was a murmur of agreement and Tom saw Dr Harker smiling through the crowd. He felt himself blushing, and looked at his shoes.

'But who could've done such a thing?' said a large woman, sobbing into a silk handkerchief.

'I dunno, Poll,' said a rat-faced man, 'but if I finds him, I'll play the surgeon with him and that's a Bible promise.'

'Not if I finds him first,' said another, pulling back his coat to show a brace of pistols tucked in his belt. 'These here pops will see the job done true.'

And so it went on. Tom listened to it all and wondered if they would ever know who had murdered Will and why. After all, if these people did not know, then who would? Tom was once again running through recent events in his mind, when he heard the grating creak of an upstairs window being opened in a house next to the churchyard.

A housemaid unfurled a Persian rug, flicking with a practised snap, tossing dust and specks of dirt into a little cloud as she did so. The brightly coloured rug shone in the greyness, swirling and shimmering as it was shaken. *Snap!* And *snap!* again. Then, as the rug was pulled back in through the window, Tom saw a man standing in the shelter of the doorway below. He was keeping out of sight as well as out of the rain. And he was watching the churchyard.

Tom wove his way through the mourners and the gravestones, trying to keep sight of the man as he did so. The drizzle and the grey gloom made it impossible to make out any of the man's features, but he was tall and broad and dressed in black.

Tom reached the path and walked briskly out through the gate and into the street. The man saw him and began to move off, bringing his hat down even further over his face. A brewer's cart passed by between Tom and the stranger; when the cart had passed, the man was gone. Tom searched the street, but there was no sign of him anywhere.

Dr Harker had come to the railings of the churchyard to see what the matter was. 'Tom!' he called. 'Is everything all right?'

'Yes,' said Tom after a moment. 'It's nothing.' He gave one last look up and down the empty street and then walked back to join the doctor.

'What's troubling you?' said Dr Harker.

'I thought I saw someone.'

'Ah, Tom,' said the doctor kindly. 'Grief can play all kinds of tricks.'

Tom guessed the doctor's meaning and shook his head. 'No, Dr Harker. Not Will. The man I saw was real enough. And he did not want to be seen.'

The doctor shot a quick glance back to where Tom had been standing. 'But you did see him, Tom? Would you know him again?'

'No, sir,' said Tom. 'He hid his face. He was a big man though – very big.'

Just then Tom and the doctor became aware of someone standing next to them. They turned and saw that it was one of the mourners; a young man, only a few years older than Tom.

'Dr Harker,' he said. 'And Master Marlowe. I have been asked to come across and give our thanks to you sirs for what you've done today. There's not many who would have done the same, and we thank you for it. I thank you for it. Will was as good as family to me and I miss him sore as burning.'

'It was the least we could do, Mr . . .'

'Carter is my name,' said the man. 'Ocean Carter.'

'Ocean,' said Tom with a smile. 'Will often talked about you, and was always singing your praises. He wanted to be like you, I think.'

Ocean's eyes loaded with tears. 'Thank you kindly, Master Marlowe,' he said.

'Call me Tom.' They shook hands.

'If I can ever be of any assistance to either of you gents, just let me know. They know me in the Red Lion Tavern in Seven Dials. You can leave a message for me there.' With that the young man turned and walked down the path and out of the churchyard.

Eventually the other mourners began to leave, each one shaking Dr Harker's and Tom's hand in turn. When they had all gone Tom turned to the doctor. 'Dr Harker, I want to thank you for all you've done for me . . . and for Will.'

'I was happy to do it, Tom,' said Dr Harker with a smile. 'I only wish I could have known Will. He was obviously quite a lad, much loved by those who knew him.'

'Yes,' said Tom. 'I think he was. He was loved.' Dr Harker patted him on the shoulder and smiled. 'I have another favour to ask of you, Doctor,' Tom went on.

'Ask away.'

'Will you help me find out who killed Will?'

Dr Harker smiled a wry half-smile, then looked up at the sky for a minute before turning back to say, 'Yes, Tom, I will. But it might be dangerous . . .'

Suddenly Tom became aware of a figure bent over Will's grave. 'Hello?' he called out nervously. The man did not reply and Tom started to walk slowly towards him. 'Hello?' he said again. The man turned to face him; it was his father.

Neither father nor son spoke for what seemed like minutes.

'Tom?' said Mr Marlowe at last.

'Father.'

'I'm not good at talking, Tom, you know that,' said his father, seemingly to his own shoes. 'I print other folks' words all day long, but the ink just seems to dry up when I try and make my own. Oh, I've got plenty of words in here,' he said, patting his chest. 'I just can't seem to get them out.'

Tom smiled. 'Let's just shake on it then, shall we, Father?'

'That would be just fine,' said his father and they shook hands. 'I must get back now, Tom – there's a lot on.' And he hurriedly stuffed a paper package into Tom's hand, tipped his hat to Dr Harker and walked briskly out of the churchyard.

Tom opened the package. Inside the paper was the pocket watch his father had given him. On the paper was printed, in an elegant typeface, the words, 'You are a good lad, Tom. Your mother would be proud of you.'

7

DEATH AND THE
ARROW CARDS

'So what shall we do first?' asked Tom impatiently a few days later, breaking the ticking silence in Dr Harker's study. The doctor sat back in his chair and put the tips of his fingers together, tapping them gently one against the other.

'Well, Tom,' he said. 'First of all we have to look at the facts at our disposal.'

'But ... But we don't have any facts,' said Tom, looking puzzled.

'On the contrary, we have lots of facts. We simply do not know, for the moment, what they mean.' Tom looked even more puzzled. 'Come, come, Tom. What do we know?'

Tom furrowed his brow and shrugged his shoulders. 'Well, I suppose we know that Will was murdered.'

'Excellent. We know that Will was murdered,' said Dr Harker, blushing slightly as he realized how harsh the words sounded. 'Sorry, Tom.'

'It's fine, sir,' said Tom, managing a weak smile. 'I know what you mean.'

Dr Harker nodded. 'But,' he went on, 'we don't know why or by whom.'

'That's what I mean,' sighed Tom. 'We don't know anything. Anything useful.'

'Ah, but we know about the card, do we not?'

'The Death and the Arrow card. Yes,' said Tom. 'We know that someone has been killing people and leaving cards on them. But how will that help us find whoever murdered Will?' Tom got to his feet and went over to the window. 'Could it have been the Mohocks?'

'I don't think so. It is beyond their wit, I think. Besides, between you and me, Tom, I think the newspapers make too much of the Mohocks. These scare stories sell papers, lad, but this is too deep for drunken rakes.' Tom looked out of the dusty windows at the sea of rooftops.

'Try to think, Tom, of anything Will might have said that could give us a clue. You told me he had a job?'

'Yes,' said Tom. 'I was, well, surprised. And he was a little put out by my surprise.'

Dr Harker smiled. 'Did he tell you what the job was?'

'No . . . He told me it was secret and that he could not tell.'

'A secret, you say?' said Dr Harker. He was playing with the curls at the end of his long powdered wig – something he always did when deep in thought. 'Did he tell you nothing about the job? Nothing at all?'

'No,' said Tom, shaking his head. 'Nothing.'

Dr Harker sighed and closed his eyes. 'No! Wait!' Tom shouted suddenly, making the doctor jump and almost tug the wig from his head. 'He did! He did say something.' He frowned with the effort of bringing back the words; the exact words. 'He said . . . he said . . . yes, that's right – he said it was the *opposite* of what he normally did.'

Dr Harker leaned forward. 'That is very interesting, Tom, is it not?'

The doctor stood up and looked out of his window. Tom was pleased to have said something of interest, but he failed to see *why* it was of interest. Dr Harker turned and, seeing the bafflement on Tom face, he smiled. 'And what was it that Will normally did?' Tom blushed. 'Come, come, Tom. It is no secret, is it? And Will was not embarrassed by his profession, now was he?'

'He was a pickpocket, sir.'

'That he was, Tom, and by all accounts a very skilled one,' said Dr Harker, patting Tom on the shoulder. 'Now what would the "opposite" of picking someone's pocket be, I wonder?'

'Putting something *into* someone's pocket?'

said Tom, who instantly felt that he had said something incredibly stupid. And when Dr Harker banged his fist down on his table, he was sure of it. But no . . .

'That's it!' cried the doctor. 'He was putting something *into* pockets. So, Tom, can that fine brain of yours hazard a guess as to what that something might be?'

'The cards!' gasped Tom, surprising himself with the thought.

'The cards.'

'But why?'

'Why indeed? Well,' said Dr Harker, sitting down once more, 'suppose you were hunting a group of men . . .'

'Hunting?' said Tom.

'Yes, hunting. Suppose you want them to know they are being hunted. You want them to fear for their lives, but you do not want to be seen.'

'I don't understand,' said Tom. 'What has this to do with Will?'

'Everything,' said Dr Harker. 'Because you hire a pickpocket – one whose skills you have seen and admired – and you get him to place cards in the pockets of the men you plan to kill.'

'Will!' exclaimed Tom.

'Precisely. The cards are designed to instil fear and panic into the recipients. They are calling cards from Death himself!'

'The Death and the Arrow cards.'

'The Death and the Arrow cards,' repeated Dr Harker, getting to his feet. 'Come, Tom. Let's take some air.'

And so the two of them left the house, walking silently together for a while in the mild spring morning, the doctor tipping his hat and saying, 'Good morning,' to passers-by, as he always did. They ambled along in no particular direction – or so Tom thought.

Finally he broke the silence. 'Dr Harker?'

'Yes, lad?'

'Do you think Will was killed by one of the men he gave a card to, or by the man he was working for?'

'I do not know,' said Dr Harker. 'There is still so much we need to discover. For instance, Tom, why do the cards show Death holding an arrow?'

'Because that is how the murderer kills his victims?' said Tom.

'Yes, yes,' said the doctor. 'But *why* does he kill them with an arrow?' Tom looked confused and Dr Harker smiled and clapped him on the back. 'If the murderer wanted to simply frighten those men, then why not simply show a figure of Death? Death can be shown with an arrow, a scythe, a sword – or nothing at all. He could have killed them in any way he chose. Using arrows seems an awful lot of trouble to go to. No, Tom – the arrow must have some significance in this whole business.'

'But what significance?' said Tom.

'We do not know. We need to find out more about the Death and the Arrow victims. They hold the secret to their murderer and to Will's.'

'But how shall we do that, Dr Harker?'

'Well, I think we may find some small degree of illumination in this establishment . . .'

Tom noticed that they were now standing outside a coffee house he had never seen before. In fact, he had been so wound up in what Dr Harker was saying, he had no idea where in the city they were.

'Remember the first victim, Tom – the man called Leech. Do you remember Purney asked – quite correctly – how it could be possible for the man to have been killed once by natives in America and then a second time, here in London?'

'Yes,' said Tom. 'But . . .'

'Well, there are few certainties in life, Tom, but one thing you can be sure of is that a man cannot be killed twice. Either he was not killed in America, or the man who was killed in London was not Leech.'

'But his own mother identified him,' said Tom.

'That she did, Tom. But was she telling the truth? Let us find out, shall we? She owns this very coffee house.'

Tom looked at Dr Harker and smiled. He really was a remarkable man. 'But how did you find her?' he asked.

'Oh, it really was not very difficult. The constable who took the details was more than happy to talk for the price of a jug of gin. Shall we go in?'

'After you, Dr Harker,' said Tom with a grin.

'Most kind, Tom,' said Dr Harker, pointing upward with his cane. 'And perhaps you might care to look at the sign on the way in.'

Tom followed the direction of the doctor's cane and there, hanging from a sinuous tangle of wrought-iron curlicues, was the coffee-house sign – a gleaming golden arrow!

8

THE ARROW COFFEE HOUSE

The clientele of the Arrow Coffee House was not as distinguished as that of The Quill; in fact several of the faces that turned to greet them as they stepped inside would not have looked out of place in the Condemned Hold in Newgate, and Tom was glad to see that Dr Harker was carrying a sword as well as a cane.

There was a furnace of a fire in the hearth and yet the room still seemed damp. The stone-flagged floor had a greenish tinge and the plaster walls were cracked and stained. The ceiling was low and made even lower by massive oak beams.

They sat down at an empty table next to the bow window and Dr Harker raised his hand for some service. A tall woman crossed the room and bid them good day. The bottom of her dress was tattered and damp where it had brushed the slimy floor.

'Well now, gentlemen, what's it to be?' she said with a crooked smile, her face whiter than her teeth.

'I shall have a coffee, and my friend here will have . . .'

'I should like a coffee also, Dr Harker,' interrupted Tom.

Dr Harker smiled. 'Very well, then. Two coffees, my good woman.'

'Two coffees it is then, gents.'

When she returned with the drinks, Dr Harker

blocked her path back to the counter. 'Tell me,' he said, 'do I have the honour of speaking to Mrs Leech?'

Her smile disappeared and was replaced by an expression more fitting to the face. 'Who wants to know?'

'Forgive me,' said Dr Harker, getting to his feet. 'My name is Dr Josiah Harker and my friend here is Thomas Marlowe. May we offer our condolences on the untimely death of your son.'

'You knew my Bill?' said the woman, looking them up and down. 'That don't seem likely, now, does it?'

'I can see you are a woman of great intelligence, and so I will get to the point.' Dr Harker pulled back a chair. 'Please . . . won't you join us? We will, of course, pay for your time.' And he produced a small velvet bag and tipped out a pile of silver coins.

'Very well, then,' said Mrs Leech, sitting down and grabbing the coins. 'Spit it out. I ain't got all day. Sarah,' she shouted, 'bring us some brandy!'

'Mr Marlowe and I are seeking information.

We are trying to identify the murderer of a friend of ours.'

'Was he shot by an arrow an' all, then?' said Mrs Leech, taking the bottle from the serving girl and pouring herself a drink.

'No . . . no, he was not. But he did have the card – the Death and the Arrow card.'

Mrs Leech took a generous gulp of brandy and stifled a sob. 'That damned card. I wish they'd never showed me it – it still gives me the shivers.' Tom knew exactly what she meant and he smiled at her in sympathy. Suddenly her face seemed to mellow a little. 'Look, I know he wasn't what you might call a *good* man, my Bill, but he was a proper son to me all the same.'

'I'm sure he loved you very much,' said Dr Harker.

Mrs Leech drained her cup and poured another. 'That he did, Dr Harker, that he did.'

'Do you think his death might have something to do with the coffee house?' asked Tom.

'The coffee house?' said Mrs Leech, looking suspicious once more.

'What with it being called The Arrow, I mean,'

said Tom. He looked at Dr Harker for support but Dr Harker's face was expressionless and his eyes were fixed on Mrs Leech.

'Oh, that,' she said, wringing her hands and trying to force a smile. 'It was Bill's idea. It was his idea of a joke.'

'A joke?' said Dr Harker.

'Oh,' said Mrs Leech nervously. 'I . . . I . . . just . . . Bill laughed at the strangest things. Of course, it wasn't so funny after all, was it, what with the way he was . . .' And she drained another cup.

Dr Harker looked about him. 'I have never come across this coffee house, Mrs Leech. Have you had it long?'

'Not long, no,' she said. 'I came into a bit of money a couple of years back – a rich uncle what died and didn't forget his little niece. I was a seamstress down Spitalfields way afore that.' She looked past them with watery eyes. 'Matter of fact, I miss it sometimes. It was hard graft, but we had a laugh, if you know what I mean. I don't know as I belong here, if you want to know the truth of it, sirs.'

'Then why—?' began Tom.

'It was Bill's idea, wasn't it? And now he's dead and I'm stuck here with these miserable so and so's. I hope you finds whoever done for Bill — and your friend.' Mrs Leech got rather shakily to her feet.

'But—' began Tom, about to tell Mrs Leech that there were *two* murders, but Dr Harker interrupted.

'It must have come as an awful shock to hear of Bill's death.'

'Yes,' said Mrs Leech wiping away a tear with her handkerchief. 'Yes . . . it was . . .'

'Especially as he was supposed to have been killed two years before . . . in the selfsame fashion.'

Mrs Leech looked up slowly from behind her handkerchief. Her eyes were cold and black, her face even whiter than before. 'Jake . . . Bull-nose . . . Skinner . . .' Each man rose at his name. 'Please show these gentlemen to the door.'

'I have a sword!' said Dr Harker, rising to his feet, but the men did not seem very impressed. Tom nudged the doctor and they backed towards the door. 'We were just leaving, weren't we, Tom?'

'Y-yes,' said Tom, standing up and joining the doctor.

The two of them edged backwards to the door, and made a hasty retreat to more familiar territory; they didn't stop until Tom finally lost the urge to look over his shoulder.

'So, Tom,' said Dr Harker as they walked through an alleyway near the Strand, 'what have we learned today?'

'To carry a loaded pistol?' replied Tom.

Dr Harker laughed and slapped him on the back. 'About the murders, Tom. What have we learned about the murders?'

Tom went over the conversation with Mrs Leech in his mind, searching in vain for something she had said that they did not already know.

'Tell me, Tom, did she seem like someone who had recently lost a son?' said Dr Harker.

'Yes,' replied Tom. 'I believe she did.'

'I agree, Tom. She may have been lying about the source of her fortune – a rich uncle indeed! –

but she was truly grief-stricken. And what does that tell us?'

Tom thought a little and then smiled. 'That the first victim was Leech.'

'Precisely! And that he died in a courtyard here in London and not in America.'

'But how could such a mistake be made?' asked Tom.

'Oh, I don't think it was a mistake, Tom. Leech *wanted* to appear dead, I'm sure of that. But why? We need to have a word with the other person who identified Leech.'

'The sergeant,' remembered Tom.

'The very same,' said Dr Harker. 'The sergeant is a link between whatever happened in America and what is happening in our city.'

'Do you think the sergeant might be one of the murderers, Dr Harker?'

'It's possible, Tom. If he is not, then he will probably be in fear of his life. And something tells me he will not want to be found. I think we are going to need some help . . .'

'You certainly are, friend,' said a voice behind them.

Tom and the doctor turned to see a thickset man tapping a cudgel against the flat of his palm.

'I have a sword!' said Dr Harker.

'D'you hear that, trooper? The gentleman has a sword!'

They turned again to find the way ahead blocked by another man, this one gaunt, with wild eyes. His head moved slowly from side to side as he spoke, like a snake about to strike. 'Well, ain't you terrified, trooper?' he called to his cohort.

'To me bones,' said the other. 'What about you?'

'Well, now, I ain't never been feared while I got these here angels to guard me.'

And with that he produced two pistols from his coat pockets and pointed them at Tom and Dr Harker.

9

OCEAN CARTER

'Say your prayers, if you're the praying kind, 'cos you are looking at your last minute on this dung heap,' said their attacker. But he had scarcely finished these words when another man came out from the shadows to stand beside him.

The man was holding a white pigeon in his hands, stroking it gently under its beak. It was Ocean Carter.

'Well, well,' he said. 'What have we here?'

'Hold it right there,' said the man, turning one of his pistols on Ocean but keeping his eyes on the doctor and Tom. 'This is no business of yours.'

'True, true,' said Ocean. 'But if it was, I find myself wondering how you would stop us all, with only two pistols.'

The man turned to face Ocean for the first time. 'Well, since you ask, brother, I would shoot you and the gentleman here, and leave the boy to my colleague.'

'Ah, but what about the pigeon?'

'The pigeon?' he snarled, but just as he did so, Ocean let the bird loose and it flapped in front of the man's face. In this split-second of distraction, Ocean lunged forward, grabbed his arm and pushed it up. The pistol fired harmlessly up into the sky. In the same instant he kicked the second pistol from his other hand and sent it clattering across the cobbles. The doctor turned and drew his sword and the man with the cudgel ran off down the alley. Meanwhile the other attacker pushed Ocean back and pulled a knife.

'The pistol, Tom,' shouted Ocean. 'To me!' Tom darted over, picked up the pistol and tossed it to Ocean, who caught it, cocked it and aimed it in one swift movement.

The attacker dropped his knife, opened up his coat and stuck out his chest, inviting the shot. 'Come on, then, bonny lad. Fire away!'

Ocean took aim.

'No!' shouted Dr Harker.

Their attacker laughed. He bowed to the doctor and walked calmly away. When he was some way off, he turned. 'If we meet again, gentlemen, I'll make you wish you'd pulled that trigger.'

'I already do!' shouted Ocean. A huge bang ripped through the alley and the attacker's hat flew off. Without stopping to retrieve it, he ran off as fast as his legs would carry him.

'What a shot!' gasped Tom.

'I'm getting old,' said Ocean, putting the smoking pistol inside his coat. 'I was aiming for his ear. Come on, gents,' he said, 'all this racket will have roused the constables. Time we wasn't here.'

He led Tom and Dr Harker briskly down several alleyways, up a curving flight of steps and through the back of an inn; to their surprise, they emerged into the busy throng of Smithfield, coming to a halt next to a wagon full of fleeces.

'You have our undying gratitude, sir,' said Dr Harker, shaking Ocean's hand.

'It was great luck that you happened by,' said Tom.

'Well, not luck exactly, Master Tom,' said Ocean. 'The truth is, I've been following you gents. I thought I might come in handy, and well, I was right.' He grinned. 'No offence intended, of course, but even with that sword, these are dangerous waters you're paddling in.'

Tom thought he saw the doctor blush slightly at the mention of his sword.

'Ocean is a very unusual name, if you don't mind me saying,' Dr Harker said.

'They call me Ocean on account of how I was born at sea; on the Atlantic's briny deep. I come into this world on a Bristol-bound brig out of the Americas, flapping on the deck like a new-caught codfish. My dear old mother, bless her bones, was returning from those parts where she'd lately resided, transported there for thievery and the like. Transported there for being poor, if you asks me. Transported there for being born in Shoreditch and not in Mayfair.' Ocean looked away for a moment and then continued. 'She died in the having of me, bless her, so I never knew her. I was adopted by another of her kind who brought me to this city and taught me the craft of thievery. That's the truth, sir. I am a thief, but I'm an honest thief.' He smiled. 'There, now you have my life.'

'And I owe you mine,' said Dr Harker, shaking his hand. 'Ocean, I'm very pleased to renew our acquaintance. And I think we ought to tell you all that we know so far, shouldn't we, Tom?'

'Yes, sir,' said Tom. 'I think we should.'

So Ocean learned of their search for Will's murderer and a little of what they had discovered so far. He was quick to offer any assistance he could, but he also had a few words of caution. 'As you found out,' he told them, 'this can be a deadly place for them that don't know their way about. You see the shape of the thieves here? Those villains would have shot you dead and thought no more about it.'

'I don't think they were thieves, Ocean. Or at least they were not about to steal from *us*.'

'How so?' asked Ocean. 'What fight could those men have had with you?'

'I don't know, Ocean,' said Dr Harker. 'But I'm sure those two men are involved in the Death and the Arrow mystery and in the murder of young Will.'

'God help them if that's true,' said Ocean. 'But there were three men in that alleyway, Dr Harker.' Tom and the doctor looked at each other in surprise. 'Four, if you count the man on the roof.'

'What do you mean?' said Dr Harker.

'Well, there was a man who didn't want to be seen, skulking in a doorway some ways off.'

'What did he look like?' said Tom, reminded of the man he saw at Will's funeral. 'Was he a big man, dressed in black?'

'Not so big, no,' said Ocean. 'Wiry, I'd

call him. Now the man on the roof – he *was* big.'

'On the roof, you say?' said Dr Harker.

'That's right. Up on the roof – behind the chimney stack. I just caught a fleeting glimpse, mind – but he was there.'

'But I've seen him too,' said Tom, suddenly remembering.

'Really, Tom?' said Dr Harker excitedly. 'Can you remember when?'

'Just after Will told me about his job, I saw someone high up on the roof ridge when there was a break in the fog. Do you think he was following Will? Is he the killer?'

'I don't know, Tom,' said Dr Harker, deep in thought. 'I don't know.' He turned to Ocean. 'Do you think you can find the men who attacked us?' he asked.

'If they can be found, I'll find them, rest assured,' said Ocean. 'But about this here army sergeant you mentioned – the one that identified the body . . .'

'Yes?' said Dr Harker.

'Well, the fact is, I've been doing some nosing around myself. A friend told me something of that soldier only this morning.'

'Well, that's marvellous, Ocean. When can we talk to this friend of yours?'

'Would now be a suitable time?' said Ocean.

'It certainly would,' the doctor replied.

'Then follow me,' said Ocean, and he was off.

Tom and Dr Harker followed on Ocean's heels, struggling at times to keep up with him. Both Tom and the doctor prided themselves on knowing London like they knew their own bedchambers, but they soon found they had not the slightest idea where they were. Ocean took them on a trail through back yards and alleyways, never once pausing to check his way; as sure as a mole in his own tunnels. A long flight of green and well-worn steps brought them to a blackened brick archway, and then all of a sudden they were in Covent Garden market, the air thick with the smell of lavender and poverty.

Outside the Green Man alehouse was a blind fiddler. Under his tattered hat was a face that had once been handsome; on his back, a moth-eaten coat that had once been the height of fashion. A red-haired boy was bending down to steal the few coins from the pewter dish at his feet, when, quick as a whip, the fiddler kicked him soundly on the backside, sending him sprawling across the pavement. Ocean picked the boy up by the scruff of his neck.

'Ocean ...' said the boy, shuffling away. 'I didn't mean no harm.'

'Be off with you, you little tick, before I kick you myself!' The boy got to his feet and scuttled off down the street.

'Ocean!' called the fiddler. 'Is that you, my friend?'

'It is, Jacob,' said Ocean. 'And I have two friends with me. They seek that soldier-boy you spoke of. They think it might help them find whoever it was that did for Will. Can you tell them what you know?'

'Well,' began the fiddler, 'I was south of the river, Southwark ways. I'd had a good day and I dropped into a tavern – the Ten-killed Cat, they call it – for a drink or two before coming back. That's when I heard him – the sergeant. He was as drunk as a watchman, and he was blathering about how he was ready for them when they came, and that no Indian was going to get the better of him.'

'No Indian?' Dr Harker repeated.

The blind fiddler nodded. 'Those were his very words. No Indian.'

'Thank you,' said Dr Harker. 'That is very interesting. Thank you for your help.' He put some money in the blind man's hand.

'With all respect, your honour, you can keep your money,' said the fiddler solemnly. 'Will was a good lad. You catch the louse what did for him, and that'll be payment enough.'

'Then will you accept our thanks?' said Dr Harker, shaking his hand.

'That I will, sir. And here's hoping you keep safe in your searching.'

'I'm beginning to wonder,' said Dr Harker as they walked away, 'if old Purney wasn't right about the Mohocks after all. In a way . . .'

10

THE TEN-KILLED CAT

The next day Tom and Dr Harker were crossing over London Bridge on their way to Southwark. When they reached the middle, they paused to take in the view: the city was bristling with church spires and wearing St Paul's like a crown. To the west the river bustled with little boats, barges and ferries. Watermen shouted, sang and cursed below them, and two young rakes cheered as they shot the rapids that formed as the mighty Thames was squeezed through London Bridge's many arches. Tom crossed to the other side to see if they had fallen in, but the skill of their boatman had seen them safely through. A group of builders on the south bank gave them a ripple of applause. One of the rakes stood up, bowed ostentatiously – and fell in, to hoots of derision. Tom laughed for the first time since Will's death.

Dr Harker put a hand on his shoulder. 'That's a view that always sets my heart to racing, Tom,' he said. He was looking past the commotion below at the mass of ships at anchor, their masts like a forest. 'The sights those ships have seen, lad: islands of ice in the cold northern seas, the pyramids of old Egypt, the temples of India – a world of wonders. Oh, Tom, would that I were a young man again, I'd sail on the next tide.'

'You're not so old, Dr Harker,' said Tom, smiling.

'Thank you for that, young Marlowe, but I fear my travelling days are behind me. When my wife was alive, I could not wait to return. Now she is dead, I have lost the urge to go. Strange, isn't it? But wherever I went, I brought something back for her – something I thought would amuse her. Without her, it seems somehow less important. She was a marvellous woman, Tom. She would have been very fond of you, I'm sure.'

'And I of her, I hope,' said Tom.

'You must remember what your father lost when your mother passed away, Tom,' Dr Harker went on. 'I know that loss and the pain of it.'

'Yes,' said Tom. 'I know it. I just wish he could . . . I don't know . . .'

'Be more like your mother?' suggested Dr Harker.

Tom smiled. 'Did you know my mother, Dr Harker?' he asked.

'I did not have that pleasure, Tom, sadly.'

Tom looked off into the distance. 'Sometimes . . .' he said with a slight choke in his voice. 'Sometimes I can hardly remember what she looked like.'

Dr Harker put an arm round Tom's shoulder. He looked back towards the ships and sighed. 'It doesn't matter if you forget her face, Tom. She's in your heart, lad. Even when I sailed away for months at a time, my Mary was always here,' he said, patting his chest. 'And she still is.'

'I wish I could sail away sometimes,' said Tom. 'You've done so much, Doctor, and I've done nothing. I've been nowhere. And I'll *never* do anything or go anywhere.'

'Come now, Tom. You're young yet, surely.'

'But that's just it,' said Tom. 'I'm young. Too young. My father would never let me go. And he needs me. He relies on me.'

Dr Harker sighed again. 'Here's my wings clipped by age and yours by youth. But still, if our wings have been clipped, there are worse perches than this, eh, Tom?' The two of them looked out, a breeze at their backs, out past the merchant fleet and the Tower of London to the river snaking its way out to sea.

Tom agreed, and they continued on their way.

They stepped off the bridge and walked along by the river, both a little nervous to be such a long way from their usual haunts. They had not gone very far before they both became aware that they were being followed.

Dr Harker turned to face their stalker. 'I have a sword!' he said grandly.

It was Ocean. 'I see you're still keeping that sword warm, Dr Harker,' he said with a grin. 'But I was thinking as how you might be needing a little company on this here jaunt.'

'We would appreciate that,' said Dr Harker, smiling.

Ocean led them along the waterfront to a building that leaned at such a precarious angle, it looked likely to fall into the Thames at any moment. Plaster had fallen from the brickwork here and there, and a hole as big as a handcart gaped in the roof.

'Here we are, gents,' said Ocean, pointing to the grimy sign above their heads. 'The Ten-killed Cat.'

An open doorway revealed a steep flight of stairs tumbling down into a basement. Tobacco smoke and the sound of tuneless singing rose from below and the three of them gingerly walked down to meet it.

It took a little while for Tom's eyes to adjust to the gloom. The gin cellar was filled with the smell of sweat and perfume and smoke, and the sound of whispering and drunken laughter. The singing they had heard came from a hollow-eyed woman near the bar, sitting with a baby at her breast.

'There's our boy,' said Ocean, pointing into the corner of the room.

Sitting at a table opposite the door was the man they had come to find. He was no longer dressed as a soldier of His Majesty's army, but wore a shabby black coat, threadbare at the cuffs, bald at the elbows. His head was bare and covered in a fine stubble; his forehead sparkled with beads of sweat. On the table in front of him, his hand rested on a loaded pistol. He never took his eyes off the door as they walked over.

'Are you Sergeant Quinn?' asked Dr Harker.

'If you didn't know, you wouldn't be asking. What do you want?'

'May we sit down?'

'You may dance like the Queen of the May so long as you do not block my view.' The three men sat down. Tom could not help following the sergeant's gaze towards the open door and the light that leaked in from it.

'We are seeking information,' said Dr Harker. 'We believe you may be of some assistance.'

'I find that very hard to believe,' said the sergeant. 'But ask away. It passes the time, and I've wanted for company these last days.'

'A friend of ours was killed. We seek his killer.'

'Do I look like a wise-woman? How would I know who killed your friend? I never saw one of you before this day and I have only recently returned to these shores.'

'It was a recent murder,' said Ocean.

'Even so . . .' said the sergeant. 'What business is it of mine? I know nothing about it.'

'This friend of ours – he had the Death and the Arrow card on him when they found him.' For the first time the sergeant looked at Dr Harker – but only for a second before returning to his vigil.

'You know something of the Death and

the Arrow murders, do you not?' said Dr Harker.

'Some,' said the sergeant, pulling a Death and the Arrow card from his pocket.

'If you know the killer,' said Tom, 'please tell us where we can find him.'

'If I knew where to find him,' said the sergeant, 'do you think I'd be sitting here waiting for him?' With that he ripped the card into pieces and tossed them onto the table next to the gun. 'And here I wait. Man or Devil or the Reaper himself, I'm ready.'

'But you think you know what he is, don't you, Sergeant Quinn?' said Dr Harker.

'And why would you say that?'

'Because you identified the body. You saw the arrow and you had seen many like it before, had you not, when you served in the Americas?'

'Who . . . Who are you – to tell me what I know?' said the sergeant.

Dr Harker reached inside his coat and, with a flourish that made everyone round the table leap back in astonishment, he produced the tip and broken shaft of the arrow given to him by Dr Cornelius.

'It was a Mohawk arrow, was it not?' he shouted and drove the point of the arrow deep into the tabletop.

11

A ROBBERY IN AMERICA

Tom, Dr Harker, Ocean and the sergeant all stared at the arrow tip jutting from the grimy wooden planking. The blade picked up the yellow glow of a nearby candle and shimmered as it trembled back and forth.

'This is the arrow that was taken from the first victim – from Bill Leech's body,' said Dr Harker. 'You knew him, did you not?'

'That I did,' said the sergeant, mesmerized by the arrowhead. 'That I did. He was trouble to me alive as well as dead. He was no more born to soldiering than I was to play the fool. Here,' he said, reaching into his pocket. 'Here's the rest of it.' Onto the table he tossed a broken arrow shaft with a set of feathered flights.

'It's a perfect match,' said Tom.

'You broke this off, did you not,' asked Dr Harker, 'when you identified Bill Leech?'

'I did. I knew that workmanship, that heathen craft. I'd seen Mohawk arrows aplenty in my time.'

'But not in London.'

'No,' said the sergeant. 'Not in London, that's very true. You've travelled in those lands?'

'I have,' said the doctor. 'Many years ago.'

'But what's all this got to do with this friend of yours that got done in?'

'It was him that put the cards in their pockets,' said Tom.

'Pickpocketry was his art,' added Ocean.

'A diver, was he?' said the sergeant. 'But was he arrowed too?'

'No,' said Tom. 'He was strangled. Please tell us what you know.'

The sergeant once again took his eyes from the doorway and looked at Tom. He smiled a wry smile and turned back. 'I do have an ache to tell someone,' he said. 'Though Lord knows, no one ever seems to benefit from the telling of the tale.'

'All the same,' said Ocean. 'Sing out. Let's hear it.'

'Very well, then,' said the sergeant. 'Leastways then when Ezekiel Quinn disappears from the world, there'll be some who know his story.' He called out for another jug of gin, and then sighed deep and long. 'So here it is, boys, the Last Dying Speech of the Condemned.' He was still looking at the entranceway but he seemed to be seeing something else.

'Well now, friends, it all goes back some years, back to the soldiering I did in the last war against the Frenchies in those godless lands across the waters.' He thanked the serving girl, who had brought him a fresh jug, and poured himself a drink. 'The savages that live in those woods are fearsome cruel, I can tell you, and the French made evil use of them in that war.' He looked at Tom. 'Be thankful that those eyes will never see the sights that these have, lad.' Tom shifted uncomfortably in his seat. The sergeant took a long drink and filled his cup again.

'Well, on with my tale. As we were in the service of the Crown, so were we in its pay. The bags of silver came all the way from England and it was given me as a duty to ensure the safe passage of this money to our troops inland. The silver was to be transported in a wagon guarded by eight outriders. I was to lead them.'

'All that silver must have been a temptation,' said Ocean.

'That it was, friend; but not to me. I was not always the fallen creature you see before you. But it was not easy to pick men for the task. I chose those I could count on in a fight, whatever else I thought of them. I even chose Shepton, God save me. A more vicious scoundrel you never did see, but what a fighter. He had a scar the whole length of his face to prove it, from his eyebrow to his jaw. An Indian tomahawk, it was. Most men wouldn't have survived it, but Shepton wasn't most men. Ah, but what a look it left him with; it made a hard face evil. No one ever forgot the sight of it.' The sergeant shook his head.

'And there was a robbery?' said the doctor.

'Of a kind, yes, there was. We were passing through forests – those forests so vast and so thick of trees, you could hide an army there unseen – when without warning an arrow struck me in the back. It hit me here, near my shoulder, and come clean through to stick out five inches from my coat.' He pulled aside his collar and filthy shirt to show the scar.

'I swung my horse round to see my men falling to the ground. I heard a shout of "Injuns!" and there was Shepton galloping towards me. When he pulls up beside me, I see he has his hand to his belly and between the fingers there juts an arrow. "Get clear!" he yells. "Save yourself! We're done for!" Then he gave my horse a slap on the rump and away I went. I thought to myself, Well, he might have been a rogue all his life, but he saved my life that day, I was sure of it.' The sergeant took another swig of gin and shook his head. 'When the troopers from the camp got there, they found every man dead – those that were there, at any rate. They'd been brutally treated . . . scalped – do you know what that means?'

'Yes,' said Dr Harker. 'The cutting off of the skin and hair from the top of the head.' Tom shuddered.

'Yes,' said the sergeant, with a grim look as if he were seeing it happen right there in front of him.

'But you said "those bodies that were there",' continued the doctor. 'Were not all the bodies found then?'

'Not all, no. Some had been taken by the savages for some devilish reason. Only their blood-soaked clothes were found.'

'How many were taken?'

'Five. Though what concern it can be of yours I cannot—'

'And was Leech one of those taken?' said Dr Harker.

'Leech? Yes. I saw him fall and thought him

dead. Somehow he must have lived. I can't say how.'

'And the silver. Was that gone too?'

'The cart was gone when my men arrived. No doubt the Indians were working for their French masters.'

'Maybe so,' said Dr Harker. 'And what action did the British army take over this incident?'

'As soon as I was able I showed one of our Indian scouts the arrow that had been pulled from me and asked him who had made it. To my surprise he said it was the work of a nearby village, the work of natives who had never given us any trouble at all. Even so, they would have to be taught a lesson. It's all these people understand, believe me.'

'You attacked the village?'

'You've seen the handiwork of those savages, sir. If we had let them go unpunished it would have sent a message to their brethren that the British army was weak.'

'So you killed them.'

'Aye.'

'Women and children as well?'

'Aye, she-savages too, and their cubs. I don't say it's wholesome work, but it's soldiering and that's that. I sleep well enough. Or at least I did.'

'Until you saw Bill Leech's body?' said the doctor.

'Until then, yes,' said the sergeant. 'I had not been in London two days when I saw him. He was alive then. At first I could not believe my eyes and so I followed him. I was conspicuous in my uniform so I was forced to hang well back. As it was he looked twitchy and nervous. He kept pulling a card from his pocket and looking at it.

'I thought I'd lost him, when I turned a corner and found myself in an empty street. Then I heard a commotion coming from a courtyard nearby. I entered it and found two men standing over Leech's body. One of the men was calling for a constable; the other was looking up – for the arrow seemed to have come from the clouds above – and saying, "It can't be, it can't be. I was right behind him when he fell." And you could see his point. There was only one exit and we stood blocking it. The courtyard was as empty as a preacher's promise.' He took another drink.

'One moment I'm following a man I thought to be arrow-shot in the Americas; the next moment he lies dead at my feet by the selfsame method, the Death and the Arrow card spilling out of his pocket.' He shook his head. 'I told the constable what I knew, and the newspapers took up the tale.'

'I think you may have known the other arrow victim,' said Dr Harker. 'He had a musket-ball wound below his right shoulder.'

The sergeant stared at him and shook his head in disbelief. 'Benjamin Cooper,' he said finally. 'Strong as an ox, he was. They pulled a ball from his back, and he didn't so much as squeak.' He shook his head again, trying to make sense of it.

'But why did you take the arrow?' said Tom.

'Ah, well, I don't rightly know,' said the sergeant. 'There's devilry here and no mistake. That arrow was Indian workmanship – Lord knows, I seen enough of it in my time. I ask you, how can that be?' When no answer came back, the sergeant wiped some beads of sweat from his forehead and licked his dry lips. 'And that ain't all. I am being followed.'

'Followed?' asked the doctor.

'I have been followed by . . . by . . . by a *some-thing*. I can't say what.'

'What do you mean?'

'Well,' said the sergeant, turning for a moment from the door to face them. 'As you ask. I fear it to be some sort of magical creature let loose on me. I fear it to be a demon.'

12

DEMON

The word 'demon' was left hanging in the air. Tom gasped and turned to look at Dr Harker, but it was Ocean who spoke first.

'A demon, you say?'

'Aye,' said the sergeant.

'You can't really believe that, surely?' said Dr Harker.

The sergeant turned on him angrily. 'Look – you know something of those people, those Indians. You know they have their magic men – the shamans—'

'Yes, yes . . . But surely—'

'They say they have the power to call upon demons to do their bidding. Well, I killed such a shaman in that raid. I run him through with my own sword. I think his demon comes now to avenge him.'

'But what makes you think you are being chased by a *demon*?' said Dr Harker.

'Because I seen him, that's why.' The three listeners leaned forward eagerly. 'I felt him watching me many times,' the sergeant explained. 'But I only seen him the once. I was walking along the Tyburn Road when I felt his eyes on me. I spun round and for some reason I looked up, just in time to see him duck down behind a chimney.' Tom gasped. The three friends all looked at each other. 'He was big, but fast with it. I don't think it was any *man* up there.' The sergeant shuddered at the recollection. 'Now I'll thank you to leave me in peace.'

'But—' began Tom.

'Leave me alone, damn you!' shouted the sergeant, banging his pistol down on the table.

'Come, Tom,' said Ocean. 'Let's get out of this crypt.'

They left the sergeant to his vigil and climbed the steps leading up to street level. A balladeer was singing a song about a highwayman and his sweetheart and they could hear cheers from the bear-baiting pit nearby.

'Come on, gents,' said Ocean. 'Let's cross back to the north shore. I never feel right south of the river.'

'I know what you mean,' said Dr Harker. 'Back to the City it is.'

'But what do you make of it all, sir?' asked Tom.

'Well, I do not believe that a demon stalks the streets of London, if that's what you mean. There is logic in all this somewhere. Some sort of *human* logic. We just need to discover it.'

'But the sergeant *saw* the attack. He saw his men killed,' said Tom.

'He saw them *fall*,' said the doctor, turning away and walking briskly on ahead. 'I do not believe that any of those missing men were actually killed, whatever the sergeant says. Do you remember what the man who attacked us called his cohort? Trooper! He called him trooper. And I do not believe that Bill Leech's mother inherited any money. I think those men stole that silver. And if I'm any judge, it is the one called Shepton who is at the bottom of it all.'

'But this Shepton, Doctor . . .' called Ocean. 'The sergeant saw him shot.'

The doctor suddenly stopped in his tracks, groaned and staggered backwards, holding his chest.

'Dr Harker?' said Tom.

Ocean grabbed hold of Dr Harker as he fell back and, as he did so, they saw an arrow sticking out from between his fingers. The two friends looked wildly about them, trying to guess from which direction the arrow might have come.

When they looked back, they found the doctor smiling.

'He saw what he was meant to see,' said the doctor, showing them the broken arrow and feathered flight the sergeant had thrown on the table. 'Seeing should not always be the same as believing, gentlemen.'

With that he set off towards London Bridge with a jaunty air, chuckling to himself, leaving Tom and Ocean staring open-mouthed.

Tom was in the printing house cleaning the blocks when Ocean burst in that same evening.

'Master Tom,' he said, 'we must get Dr Harker and go back to the Ten-killed Cat. I tipped the landlord some silver to tell me if anything happened to the sergeant and he's sent word. Something's happened, Tom. He says he'll leave things be until we get there, so long as we're quick. Will you come?'

'Of course,' said Tom. 'I must just tell my father, and then I'll be with you directly.'

But when he heard where his son was intending to go, Mr Marlowe looked worried. 'Tom,' he said, 'I know you feel a need to find the men who murdered young Will Piggot, but . . .' He looked down at the floor, then banged his hand down on the printing press. 'You're all I have, Tom!'

'I have to do this, Father,' said Tom.

His father sighed. 'I know it, Tom. I admire you for it. But take care.'

'I will, Father, I will.'

Tom's father patted him on the shoulder and Tom left the print room.

Ocean was about to follow him out when Mr Marlowe grabbed him by the coat. 'You take care of that boy, do you hear me?' he said.

'No harm will come to Tom if I have any say in it,' said Ocean.

'I'll hold you to that,' said Mr Marlowe.

'I'd expect you to,' said Ocean.

Dr Harker was as keen as Tom to discover what had happened in Southwark, but none of them were keen to reacquaint themselves with either the sergeant or the gin-cellar he was holed up in. Ocean whistled to a hansom cab, and it pulled up in front of them.

'The Ten-killed Cat in Southwark,' said Ocean. 'And straight there, mind. We ain't Italians.'

'I don't go south of the river,' protested the driver. 'Not at this hour . . .'

'Get in,' said Ocean to Tom and Dr Harker.

'Hey!' shouted the driver.

'Drive on, you rogue, or my friend here, who is a Member of Parliament, will see to it that you lose your licence – if you have one, that is!'

After a few seconds' thought the driver moved off, muttering to himself about the unfairness of life and the troubles that cursed him – as cab drivers often do. Tom and Dr Harker smiled in admiration at Ocean's quick wit, and he smiled back, enjoying the praise.

'A Member of Parliament, eh?' said Dr Harker.

'And a fine one you'd make, I'm sure,' said Ocean with a grin. Tom laughed.

'A little less from you, lad,' said the doctor. 'I had half a thought to go into politics when I was younger.'

'Well, we're all thankful you had a change of heart, Doctor, for a greater set of rogues and thieves you couldn't find outside of Newgate.' Dr Harker smiled. 'It's no life for an honest man, like yourself.'

The cab pulled up outside the Ten-killed Cat, the driver still muttering to himself, and Tom, Ocean and Dr Harker got out and stood on the pavement underneath the creaking sign.

'Wait here till we return,' said Ocean to the cab driver.

'Ten minutes and no more,' he replied.

They walked down the steps as before. The sergeant was just where they had left him. His eyes were still fixed on the door, his hand holding his pistol, the torn pieces of card lying next to it.

But on his coat was another Death and the Arrow card, pinned there by the arrow that jutted from his chest.

13

ECLIPSE

It was only a day after the trip to Southwark
and the discovery of the sergeant's body that
Ocean brought news of another victim. Dr
Harker went to view the body at Dr Cornelius's
invitation. It turned out to be the man who had

attacked them after their visit to the Arrow Coffee House. If Dr Harker was right, then that meant there were only two of the men left.

April 22 was the day of the eclipse and Tom set out along Fleet Street with a parcel of pamphlets to deliver on his way to Dr Harker's house. He and Ocean had been invited to view the spectacle from the doctor's roof. A strange evening twilight was spreading over the city, even though it was eight o'clock in the morning, and birds, in their confusion, were heading home to roost.

Tom walked briskly, eager not to miss anything and glad to have something to think about other than the grim business of the past few days. Without warning, a man stepped out in front of him and blocked his way. 'What's the hurry, lad?' he asked. Then Tom recognized him – the man with the cudgel who had attacked them in the alley when they emerged from the Arrow Coffee House. A second man stepped out of the shadows. He had a long white scar running down the length of his face; a face every bit as evil as the sergeant said it was.

'Shepton!' said Tom, instantly regretting that he had let the name escape.

'Hark, Fisher!' said Shepton with a grin. 'He knows my name.'

'And now he knows mine, thanks to you.'

'No matter,' said Shepton. 'He shan't tell, shall you, lad?'

Tom threw the parcel in Fisher's face and ran down the street, with the two men in loud pursuit.

'Stop, thief!' cried Shepton. 'He has my watch!'

A passer-by made a lunge for Tom, but he swerved round him and ducked down an alley-way, only to find a dead end. Shepton and Fisher appeared at the entrance, silhouetted against a pale grey sky.

'Well now, this is a much quieter place for a quiet chat,' said Shepton. 'Look at him, Fisher. We've gone and frightened the poor mite. Calm yourself, lad. We just want to talk, that's all. I promise you I'll not hurt you. We just want to know what that crazy soldier told you before he was so *brutally* dispatched.'

'He said he thought he was being followed by a demon,' said Tom.

Shepton laughed loudly. 'Do you hear that, Fisher? A demon! He was a bigger fool than we took him for.'

'The boy knows nothing. Let's just kill him and be done,' said Fisher. 'All this talk makes me ache.'

'Fisher!' shouted Shepton and pushed him out of the way. 'Take no heed, son. You'll come to no harm from me, I swear it. Now, what else did our brave sergeant tell you?'

'He thought that you were dead. That you had saved his life,' said Tom. Shepton laughed again. 'But Dr Harker knew it was a trick!' said Tom. 'He knew you stole the silver.'

Shepton grabbed Tom by the collar and pulled him close. 'Oh dear me,' he said. 'Here I am, talking all friendly like, and there you are talking me to the gallows. But I promised you I'd not hurt you, and I'm a man of my word.' He smiled once more and then his face became blank. 'Kill him, Fisher.'

At that moment a maid opened a door into the alley and Tom bundled past her and into the house. The maid screamed, but Tom ran through the hall and out of the front door, onto the street. He could hear Fisher close behind and he ran without giving thought to the direction.

'Stop, thief!' called Fisher, using the same trick as Shepton. Tom ducked down an alleyway to avoid a butcher's boy who tried to block his path with a cart. Fisher was only fifty yards behind him as he tumbled out in front of St Paul's Cathedral.

As Fisher started to catch up with him, Tom ran hell for leather up the cathedral steps. Fisher lunged for him, but missed and fell, cursing his prey and rubbing his bruised knee. Tom ducked between the massive stone columns of the west front and in through the open door.

He felt more exposed than ever in the vastness of the cathedral. The scale of the building only served to make him feel more vulnerable. It seemed to take an age to reach the cover of a stone pillar; he ducked behind, hoping Fisher had not seen him.

Fisher entered the cathedral like a thunderclap; his boot heels clattered on the stone floor, echoing round the cavernous nave, then squeaked to a halt. Tom dropped silently to the floor and began to crawl away from the sound. There was a group of gentlemen only a few yards away. If he could just reach them, he would be safe. Fisher would not kill him with witnesses.

'I am a constable,' shouted Fisher, his voice booming round the building. 'I do not wish to alarm you but there is an escaped felon in the cathedral. He is a convicted murderer, but he is but a boy and armed only with a butcher's knife. Could any of you good gentlemen assist me?' Just as Fisher had known it would, the cathedral emptied in seconds.

''Tis just the two of us now, boy!' he shouted. 'And what better place to meet your maker?'

Tom crawled away from the voice. His breath roared in his ears like a storm and his heart seemed to be booming out in the silence. *Silence!* Tom suddenly realized that he could no longer hear Fisher's footsteps. Somehow the silence seemed more dreadful.

He held his breath and peeped round the base of a column. There was no one there. He retreated behind the column again, fighting to catch his breath. The door seemed so far away, but he must try and reach it; he might not get another chance. He got to his feet and looked again; still no Fisher. He took a deep breath and ran towards the door.

Tom had not run two yards before a foot shot out from behind a column and sent him sprawling across the floor. It was Fisher. He strode forward and, in one movement, dragged Tom to his feet. He pulled the boy towards him by his lapels with one hand, holding an open clasp knife in the other. Tom could see his own frightened face reflected in its blade.

Fisher smiled and Tom brought his knee up with as much force as he could muster, hitting his attacker solidly between the legs. Fisher groaned and cursed and loosened his grip on Tom just enough for him to break free and run. But Fisher still blocked the exit; Tom was forced to run back into the cathedral.

Pain slowed Fisher down for a few seconds but anger is a powerful anaesthetic and he was furious. He was soon only yards behind Tom, who feared he was now trapped; but then he saw an open door and made a dash for it. Fisher was after him immediately.

The door opened onto a spiral staircase and Tom ran up the steps, two at a time. He could hear Fisher at his heels and his breath came in gasps, the muscles in his legs begging him to stop, but fear and will-power urged him onward and upward.

His heart was thumping against his ribcage as he burst through a door which led out onto a circular gallery inside the dome. Tom looked over the balcony to see the sunburst pattern in the stone floor far below. He pulled himself back from the edge, dizzy with vertigo and breathlessness.

'Where now, boy?' said Fisher as he too emerged into the gallery.

Tom did not wait to answer, but set off through another door and found himself climbing yet more steps, climbing for all he was worth in the dark, with Fisher scrabbling up behind him. Tom could hear his breath as he made for a small door ahead of him.

As he opened it, he gasped with the realization

that he was now at the top of the dome, on a tiny parapet looking down on the whole of London spread out below him. But even more extra-ordinary than this was the incredible spectacle taking place in the sky above.

Suddenly, Fisher grabbed him. 'Now, lad,' he said. 'Let's see if we can't find you a quicker way down.' But then he too became aware of the otherworldly darkness. 'What the . . .?'

The sun turned black and the shadow of the moon rushed towards them across the hills and over London, until it plunged the city into another night. Tom and Fisher both stared in wonder as a luminous ring appeared around the black disc of the moon, a weird mother-of-pearl glow.

Flashes of light shot out and shimmered and then the edge of the moon turned blood-red. Both hunter and prey were rooted to the spot with some kind of animal terror, but it was Tom who came to his senses first.

He pushed Fisher away and shrugged off his grip. Fisher, still mesmerized by the eclipse, staggered backwards, correcting his balance too late to stop himself flipping over the railing. He screamed out as he slithered down the curving roof, bouncing once before he plummeted out of sight.

Tom made his way down to ground level and managed to slip away as a small crowd gathered round Fisher's body. Someone shouted out that he had the Death and the Arrow card on him, and more people ran up to take a look.

Tom walked through the gloomy streets as the sun began to reappear from behind the moon. Sparrows began to twitter and pigeons coo at this false dawn, and church bells rang out in celebration of the world's return to daylight.

However, Tom's only thought was to reach Dr Harker's house safely, and he walked the whole way in dread of seeing Shepton's evil face appear in front of him again.

'Tom?' said Dr Harker, when the maid had showed him up to the roof. 'Whatever became of you?'

Tom fought to catch his breath, then told the doctor and Ocean about his escape.

'Good Lord,' said Dr Harker. 'This must end,

Tom. There is too much danger. You could have been killed.'

'No!' shouted Tom. 'Not now. I have to know what happened to Will. I won't have Will's life forgotten, and neither you nor my father nor anyone else will stop me.'

14

THE DOOR IN THE ROOF

Tom and Dr Harker were alone in the courtyard – alone, that is, apart from a rat, which
hurried away at their approach and scuttled out
of sight behind a woodpile. A window creaked
open above them and a maid sang quietly and

tunelessly from inside. Dr Harker looked about him. He had brought Tom to the scene of the first Death and the Arrow murder, to see if they could find any clues to what had happened there.

'So, Tom, what do you see?'

'Well, sir,' said Tom, 'it's as they said. There is but the one entrance behind us, and anyone escaping that way would be seen.'

'That's true, Tom,' said Dr Harker. 'We are surrounded by buildings on all sides. There are three doors, as you see, but all three are locked and bolted from the inside. The unfortunate Leech could have been shot from one of those windows, of course, but the occupants are lawyers, men of high standing, and there was no report of an intruder.'

'Then how . . .?'

'How indeed?' smiled Dr Harker. He put his hand on Tom's shoulder. 'Remember our visit to Dr Cornelius?'

'Yes, Doctor,' said Tom, and he shuddered slightly at the memory. 'Of course.'

'Remember the body, Tom. Remember what Dr Cornelius said about the arrow.'

Tom tried to remember. 'I think he said the arrow was angled as if it came from above.'

'Good, Tom. That he did,' said Dr Harker. 'Now, what of the sergeant? Do you remember what he said?'

Tom half-closed his eyes and looked down at his feet, deep in thought. 'Yes,' he said suddenly. 'He said that it was as if the arrow came from the clouds.'

'Excellent! He did,' said Dr Harker, pointing upward. 'The arrow, it seems, came from above.'

'But from where, sir?' said Tom, confused. 'You said it could not have come from the windows.'

'Not from the windows, Tom,' said Dr Harker. 'From the roof!'

Tom looked up. From where they were standing there was hardly any view of the roof at all, but he could see enough to know that it was too steep for a man to stand on without sliding off to his death. He turned back to Dr Harker to find that he was knocking at one of the courtyard's three locked doors.

'Good day,' said the doctor with a bow as the

door was opened. A pale and gaunt-looking clerk eyed him suspiciously through a narrow gap. 'I have Mr Garrison's kind permission to gain access to the roof.'

'Yes . . .?' said the clerk, without opening the door further.

'Then would you be so kind as to show my young friend the way?'

'Me, sir?' said Tom, a little nervously. He was not keen either to enjoy a further acquaintance with the skeletal clerk, or to test his head for heights once more so soon after his experience on the dome of St Paul's.

'Would you, Tom? Splendid!' Somehow Tom seemed to have volunteered without knowing it.

The clerk opened the door a little further, but Tom still had to squeeze through. 'Take the stairs to the top of the house,' he was instructed. 'There you will find a door barred by three bolts. Mind your step as you leave it or it will be your last.'

'Thank you,' said Tom, but the clerk had not finished.

'Do not enter any other door. Do not touch anything you may find on the way. Re-bolt the roof door on your return.' With that, the clerk walked away down the hall.

Tom looked up at the dimly lit stairwell and began to climb. At each flight the house appeared more and more unused, and a cloud of dust rose with his every step. Cobwebs tickled his face and piles of yellowing papers clogged the landings. The treads creaked like the planks of a ship and the rotten banister swayed at his touch.

When Tom reached the top of the staircase, there was, just as the clerk had described, a small but heavy oak plank door, bordered by metal bands bolted to the wood and fixed in place by three massive steel bolts.

The first two bolts moved readily enough, but the third seemed as if it had not been moved since the day the door was hung. Tom had to brace himself against the wall with his feet and use all his strength to shift it. Finally, with one huge last effort, he freed it and lifted the latch. He was thankful to the clerk for his warning: the door opened up onto a treacherously steep roof, and had he stepped out onto those greasy tiles, he felt sure that it would indeed have been his last step.

To make matters worse, the opening was not above the courtyard, but above the alley on the other side of the building. To gain any view at all of the courtyard would mean climbing over the roof. Tom hesitated and made to go back downstairs. Then he thought of Will and looked back up at the roof ridge.

He edged out of the door and immediately lost his footing, sending a tile skittering down onto the street below. There was a distant crash, a distant curse. He gripped the doorframe for all he was worth.

The doorway was housed in a small projection from the main body of the roof, and Tom managed at length to scrabble on top of it. Kneeling precariously, he used this as a platform from which to reach the summit. He flung an arm over the roof ridge and then a leg. Soon he sat straddled across it as if he were riding a donkey. A crow eyed him curiously from its perch on a chimneypot.

Tom called down to the doctor way below him in the courtyard.

'Tom!' he heard in reply. 'Be careful, lad!'

'I will! It's a fine view!' he shouted, trying to sound more relaxed than he was.

'What can you see? Is there space for a man to hide or stand?'

'No, Doctor,' called Tom. 'There are only the chimney stacks.' He looked down. 'Wait – there is a ledge of sorts at the base of the roof, but it can only be a few inches wide.'

'But could a man walk along it if it were on the ground?' called Dr Harker.

'If it were on the ground, I could walk on it,' called Tom. 'But it is a hundred feet up!'

'Then we are looking for a murderer with a head for heights!'

'A tightrope walker!' shouted Tom, with a sudden flash of inspiration. Of course! He had seen dozens of them. They could walk along a length of rope as easily as if they were strolling the pavement.

'Perhaps,' said Dr Harker, deep in thought. 'Now, come down before you fall down, lad.'

Tom didn't need to be asked twice. He swung one leg over the roof ridge and scuttled down towards the door on his heels and backside. As he clambered round to re-enter the doorway he thought he heard a noise behind him. He was about to turn round when something was put over his head, plunging him into darkness, and he was lifted off his feet and carried away across the rooftops.

15

CAPTURED

Tom was carried for some time, aware in spite of his hood of the amazing agility of his captor. This man might indeed be a tightrope walker. But there was something else about him — so agile and yet built powerfully enough to carry

Tom as if he were nothing more than a rag doll. Tom could sense the sureness of his tread. He had struggled at first, but soon realized that it would not be in his interests to force the man to stumble.

Eventually Tom was set down. He was seated, his back resting up against some support, his legs stretched out together straight in front of him. Before he could move, something was tied firmly around his waist and then around his wrists and feet.

'Who . . . Wh-who are you?' stuttered Tom. There was no reply. 'Why have you brought me here? Please, sir.' Again there was no reply. He made a few more attempts at contact, but each one met with the same stony silence. As he spoke the fabric of the hood caught between his lips. He pulled at it a little more until he had it between his teeth, then tugged a little; the hood began to move. He lowered his head to allow the hood free movement and worked it down a little more. No one tried to stop him so he carried on. Inch by laborious inch he nibbled and tugged, until all at once the hood fell down in front of his face and he let out a cry of terror.

He was tied to the charred roof beam of a large house. The house had once had four storeys, but had been gutted – probably in the Great Fire some fifty years earlier. Not a floor remained to break Tom's view of the rubble-strewn basement far below him.

He gasped and his heart beat wildly. He pressed back against the wall but he was so securely tied he could not move more than an inch in any direction. He yelled out, 'Help! Somebody! Help!' but no one came. He could not move, but neither could he fall. At least he was safe from that immediate danger. But what of his captor? Who and where was he? And what fate awaited Tom on his return?

These thoughts and many others swirled around Tom's mind as day gave way to evening and evening to night. He called out every now and then, but to no avail, and despite all his efforts to stay awake, as a full moon rose between the skeleton of roof beams and trusses, he fell fast asleep.

It seemed only seconds later when he opened

his eyes, but it was now dawn and a strange pinkish light washed over his prison, making it somehow seem even stranger and more terrifying. Then he heard a noise from the foot of the building.

He looked down to see a figure far below him; it was a man in black, wearing a three-cornered hat and tumbling periwig. Tom was about to shout out when the man began, with astonishing speed and sure-footedness, to climb up the wall. He began to wonder if the sergeant had not been right after all when he claimed that this was not a man, but some kind of demon.

In no time at all the man appeared on one of the beams at the opposite gable end of the building to the beam to which Tom was tied. There seemed no way for the man to cross the gap between them, for the beams ran cross-wise, not along the length of the house.

As Tom was considering this, the man pulled himself up one of the rafters and onto the ridge beam to which all the rafters rose. Tom thought of his own fear sitting astride the ridge tiles of the lawyer's house, and marvelled at the fearlessness of his captor. The man got to his feet and walked along the beam, as untroubled as if he were strolling along a wide city street. He never once paused for balance, but walked steadily and gracefully, looking straight ahead until, in one easy movement, he dropped down in front of Tom.

A rafter blocked Tom's view of the man and, try as he might, he could not move enough to catch even a glimpse of him. He could see his captor's feet, though, and noticed he was wearing the strangest shoes. They were made of some kind of pale leather, minutely decorated with tiny coloured beads and patterned stitching. He had seen something of the kind before, but he could not remember where.

'Why do you follow me?' asked the man suddenly in an accent Tom had never heard before.

'I'm not. I mean, I . . . I . . . I was searching for my friend's murderer,' said Tom bravely.

'And you thought I was that man?'

'I don't know,' said Tom, still trying to get a proper look at the stranger. 'We did not know who we were looking for. But in any case, now I know who it was who killed my friend.'

'Shepton?' Tom could hear the hatred in the man's voice.

'You know him?'

'Yes, I know that devil. I have been searching for him this very night,' said the man. 'And this friend he killed? This friend was Will Piggot, I think.'

'You knew Will?' exclaimed Tom.

'I did know him. Was proud to know him. Such skill in one so young. I only caught him picking my pocket by accident. I never saw such swiftness of hand, such quick wits. What a hunter he would have made. I watched him work the crowd for an hour before I spoke to him.'

'It was you who paid him to put the Death and the Arrow cards in those men's pockets! It's your fault he's dead!' shouted Tom.

There was no reply. Tom feared for his life again and wished he had held his tongue.

'Yes,' said the man at last. 'I am to blame, as sure as if I had strangled him myself, and I'm sorry for it. It gives me another sorrow in a life of sorrows, and another reason to look for Shepton's death. Now there are only two of them left. He and the one called Fisher. They are the last.'

'No,' said Tom. 'Fisher is dead.' He told him about the attempt on his life and of Fisher's fall to his death.

The man crouched down and began to untie the ropes from around Tom's ankles. Tom could still not see his face beneath the brim of his hat. When his feet were free, he momentarily considered kicking out at his captor, but his hands were still tied, and who knew if anyone would ever find him?

Tom let his legs drop on either side of the beam, welcoming the chance to move and shake off some of the damp chill of the night. His captor stooped over him holding a huge knife and Tom cried out in fear of his life; however, the knife was used to cut not Tom's throat, but the rope holding him to a metal bracket behind his head. He was grateful to be released, but instantly felt even more aware of the drop below.

'I have food. Eat.'

The man tossed a leather bag into Tom's lap. It was decorated in a similar way to the beaded shoes. Again Tom tried to remember where he had seen that decoration before. He reached inside the bag and found a small loaf and a hunk of cheese. He took hearty bites out of both.

Meanwhile, his captor took off his hat and wig, tucking them into the space between wall and rafter by Tom's head. He then dropped down to sit astride the beam opposite him. Tom gasped in amazement.

Most men in London shaved their heads and stuck their wigs to their scalps, but unlike other men, this man had a ridge of hair running from the top of his head to the nape of his neck, tied at the back with a single black feather. But more, much more extraordinary than this, his face and neck were decorated with strange patterns not unlike those on his shoes. Silver triangles hung from his earlobes. The sergeant's talk of demons flooded back into Tom's mind.

'Wh— Wh-what are you?'

'I am Tonsahoten.'

16

TONSAHOTEN

'You are an Indian?' said Tom, now more excited than scared.

'Your people call me such – and worse. Mohawk is what I am.'

Now Tom remembered where he had seen

decoration like that on the Indian's shoes – Dr Harker had shown him shoes like that. He called them 'moccasins'.

'I had never thought to meet a sav—' Tom winced and eyed the Mohawk nervously.

Tonsahoten smiled. 'Yes. You call us "savages",' he said with a sigh. 'And yet I have seen what the white men are. I have seen what white men do.'

'But why are you here? How did you get here?'

'I came here in search of the men who killed my family, who killed my people.'

'The sergeant!' said Tom. 'He told us that he attacked a village. He thought those people had killed his men and robbed the army. Was that your village?'

'Yes,' said Tonsahoten. 'My village. My mother. My father. My sister. My people. Only I escaped.' He looked away. 'They are all gone. My life is gone now. Yes – I killed the sergeant.'

Tom could think of nothing to say, but all fear had gone now; only pity remained.

The Mohawk hung his head. 'It happened some years ago. White men had brought their wars to my country again, and again my people had allowed themselves to become a part of it. Some of us fought for the French against the English, some for the English against the French. We allowed ourselves to be bought for guns and whisky, while piece by piece the white man took our land, cut down our forests.'

He stopped and looked at Tom. 'But even so, we lived as peaceably as we could, ignoring the taunts of the drunken English soldiers who were camped near our village. Then one day I was hunting on my own in the great wood and I saw them – a group of soldiers. One of them – the one we now know as Shepton – had a bow, and was practising firing arrows into a tree. I had heard that a soldier was paying for lessons in the bow and here he was. He was good. He rarely missed. The soldiers cheered each time the arrow struck home, and then they gathered together in a huddle and began to talk in whispers too quiet to hear. I tried to move closer, but a jay set up a cry and gave me away. They picked up their guns and I fled.

'I thought no more about it until some days

later, when I saw the same men riding through the woods on the trail heading north. They formed part of a group of eight outriders guarding a wagon. The sergeant led the group. There was a kind of ditch not far from the trail, and I could walk alongside unseen.

'All of a sudden, Shepton, who was riding towards the back of the group, made a sign with his hand. He and four others reached into the back of the cart and pulled out bows and a quiver of arrows. The men took an arrow each.

'They were so close to their targets they could not miss. Two of the men shot the driver and his guard, and another two shot the two riders ahead of them. Shepton had the hardest shot, and he appeared to have missed because he only hit the sergeant in the shoulder. But this was intentional. He wanted a witness who would say for sure that it was an Indian attack.'

'Sergeant Quinn,' said Tom.

'Yes,' said Tonsahoten. 'Shepton shouted, "Injuns!" and kicked his horse forward, pretending to have been shot himself. He told the sergeant to get clear, and slapped his horse.'

'So the sergeant would think Shepton had saved his life,' said Tom.

The Mohawk nodded. 'As soon as the sergeant was out of sight, the robbers finished off the soldiers they had shot and then, taking tomahawks from the back of the wagon, they scalped them.' Tonsahoten saw the look of shock on Tom's face and smiled grimly.

'They hurriedly changed out of their bloody clothes and ripped them and scattered them about in the woods for the English to find when the sergeant reported the incident. Then, with a great whoop, they made off with the wagon at great speed.

'I did not wait for the soldiers to find the bodies. I could see what they would think, what they were meant to think. The arrows used were from my own village, and I ran to warn the elders of the danger to our people.

'But they would not listen. I was young, they said. The English would listen to us, they said. And when nothing happened, when no soldiers came, I began to believe that they were right. But it was not to be.' Tonsahoten looked down and shook his head, unable to speak for a few moments.

'A week or so later, the soldiers came, very early, before the hunting party had left the village. At their head was the same sergeant who had been with the other soldiers. He looked pale and his left arm hung down by his side, bandaged under his uniform.

'The shaman from our village – our priest – walked slowly towards him and asked him what he wanted. The sergeant took out his sword and ran it through his chest. Then the soldiers began shooting.

'I ran for my bow, but a soldier blocked my way; I turned to run, but was confronted by another. He struck me with the butt of his rifle and I fell to the ground. He split open my head and blood flowed down my face and neck. The blood and my lifeless appearance saved me from the bayonet that would surely have followed. But when I saw what lay around me, I began to wish I had been killed.

'My mother, who had never harmed anyone in her life, was dead. My lovely sister . . . my father, who taught me to hunt and to fish . . . my friends, my whole village – all dead. All dead. All dead . . .' Tonsahoten broke off from his story and hung his head.

'I'm sorry for it,' said Tom after a little while, but still the Mohawk did not reply. They sat in silence for several minutes until Tonsahoten finally spoke again.

'I tell you all this so that you will leave this hunt. Shepton is the man you seek, but he is mine, promised to me by my oath. Nothing must stand in my way.' The words hung in the air between them, part threat, part warning. Then the Mohawk took a quick look around and said, 'Come, I will see you safely home.'

Tonsahoten replaced his wig and hat, and carried Tom down from the high beam. As they walked through the city, the Mohawk kept his head bowed to hide the markings on his face. His bow and arrows were in a long leather bag thrown over one shoulder. He was far less notice-able than many of the strange inhabitants of the City of London.

When they reached the alleyway leading to the

Lamb and Lion printing house, Tonsahoten bid Tom farewell. He turned to leave but, as he did so, his way was blocked and four pistols were pointed at his head. Tom suddenly saw that Dr Harker was standing nearby with his father.

'I am Under-marshal Hitchin,' said one of the men. 'You are under arrest.' He struck him in the stomach with a short staff.

'No!' shouted Tom. 'Don't hurt him!'

'What do we have here?' said Hitchin, ignoring Tom and pulling off the Mohawk's wig. 'Some sort of cannibal, here in our fair city.'

The Mohawk stared impassively into Hitchin's eyes and the under-marshal moved to hit him again.

'Execute your duties fairly or the mayor will hear of it,' warned Dr Harker.

Hitchin did not acknowledge the doctor, but he did not hit the Mohawk again. 'Take him away,' he said with a smile, then tipped his hat at Tom's father. 'Mister Marlowe.' He turned to Tom. 'Master Marlowe. You continue to keep strange company. I shall have to keep my eye on you.'

'Don't you dare to talk to my son like that!' said Mr Marlowe.

'My apologies, if I caused any offence. To be sure, this savage is a vast improvement on that flea-bait Piggot.'

Tom lurched forward but his father caught him by the arm. Hitchin smiled again and walked away, as Tonsahoten was put in chains and thrown into a carriage bound for Newgate.

Dr Harker stepped forward and greeted Tom with relief. 'Your father sent for a constable when I told him you'd gone missing. We feared for your life. Hitchin got to hear of it and wanted to grab some glory. What a vile creature he is. I think I shall be keeping *my* eye on *him*.'

'Thank God you're safe at any rate, Tom,' said Mr Marlowe. 'I thought I'd lost you.'

'I'm fine, Father,' said Tom, watching the carriage disappear into the distance. What was going to become of the Mohawk now?

17

BOUND FOR ENGLAND

Tom and Dr Harker took their place in the queue outside Newgate prison. As always, it contained a motley collection of people. They paid their entrance money and stepped into the raucous world of the Common Ward.

Inmates and their visitors were drinking at the bar and a fight was erupting in the corner over a game of dice. Pigeons cooed from their perches and flitted in and out of the open windows. A pig trotted past, chased by a one-eyed dog.

A flight of stairs took them to the Stone Hold, where they found the Mohawk crouched in the gloom. His feet and hands were manacled and chained to the floor, his head was bare and he stared ahead with a fixed expression. He did not acknowledge their presence.

The turnkey gave him a prod with the toe of his boot. 'Visitors, you heathen scum,' he said. Tonsahoten turned and slowly rose to his feet. The turnkey shrank back towards the door. 'Heathen scum,' he muttered from a safer distance. The Mohawk returned to his previous stance.

Then, to Tom's surprise, Dr Harker began talking in the strangest way. Tom was about to ask if he was all right, when Tonsahoten turned and began to respond in kind. Something approaching a smile began to appear on his face.

'You speak my language?' said the Mohawk.

'A little,' said the doctor.

'You speak it well, but for the boy's benefit, we should speak English, I think.'

'I am Dr Harker,' said the doctor, offering his hand. 'Tom here you already know.'

Tonsahoten shook his hand and got to his feet. Again Tom was struck by his size, especially in this confined space. 'How do you come to know my language?' asked the Mohawk.

'I travelled in your lands for some time in my younger days. How do you come to know ours?'

Tonsahoten smiled. 'The boy has no doubt told my tale,' he said. The doctor nodded. 'Well, I vowed that I would avenge my family, my people. I left my home – the woods I had loved so much – and I became a seafaring man. The white men set great store by my head for heights and set me to work at the top of the main-mast, looking for whales on the far horizon. When I saw one of those great beasts I would shout out and then scramble down to the deck and into the long-boats, ready for the chase. When my job as lookout was done, I turned harpooner, standing in the prow to do battle with those giant fish. It was dangerous work. I saw men snapped like tinder wood by a flick of their tails.' Tom's eyes widened at every word the Mohawk spoke.

'I learned your tongue, and many others. The sea life is open to all, and I struck up friendships with men from all nations. Had I not vowed to search out my people's killers, I would never have left that life. I might have been happy there.'

'And how did you find them? Shepton and the others?' asked Dr Harker.

'By chance,' said the Mohawk. 'I had made my mind up to come to London. I had a desire to see the great city I had heard so much about. I left my whaler in Nantucket and signed on as crew aboard a ship carrying tobacco, bound for England.

'On reaching London, I quit my ship and set out to see the sights with two shipmates. We had not walked far when one of my companions pointed to a coffee house and said, "That's the place for you, Tonsa!" This on account of the golden arrow for its sign.

'I smiled at his joke and would have thought no more of the Arrow Coffee House if a man I recognized had not walked out of the door. It was one of the soldiers from the robbery. The one called Leech.

'A rage welled up in me. I had sworn to myself that if ever I should see any of those men again I would kill them on the spot. My friends saw the look on my face and asked me what the matter was. The one who had made the joke thought that I had taken offence. I told him that I had something I needed to do and that I would meet them later.

'They parted company with me and I stood there, filled with violence. I followed Leech and had to stop myself from killing him there and then. But I knew that if I killed Leech I might never see the others. And I wanted the others too.' The Mohawk's voice had lowered as he spoke of the soldiers and he growled these last words out.

'But I was not dressed for London. Even in this city of misfits I stood out, and people stared as I walked by. My head was still bare, for one thing, so my first stop was a wig shop. The man who served me looked a little surprised to have my custom – as though I might eat him at any moment. But he took my money all the same.

'And I had plenty of money. I had earned a great deal on the whaler, for I took a share in each whale I spotted and each I helped to catch – and we caught many whales. I used the money to buy the wig, my hat, my coat and breeches, my shoes and stockings – all the strange womanish garb you white men clothe yourselves in.' Tom smiled at Dr Harker, who pretended not to notice and played with the ends of his wig.

'I knew that if I watched the Arrow Coffee House long enough, I might see the other robbers, and sure enough they came. I found that I could watch unseen from the rooftops of the city and I decided to panic them a little, as you might a herd of deer. That is where the cards came in. I had them printed here in the city. I made the printer a drawing of an image I remember seeing a shipmate carve into a whale tooth. All that was left was to deliver them. And that is where Will Piggot came in.'

'But why Will?' said Tom.

'I noticed Will picking pockets and saw his skill,' said Tonsahoten. 'I gave him money and he put the first card in Leech's pocket. He set off to plant the other cards as I followed Leech from the rooftops. It was a cold day and Leech put his hands in his pockets – and found the card.

'At first he was confused. I saw him look at the card and turn it over, trying to think how it might have come to be in his pocket. Then I called out to him. He looked up and saw me standing high above him, my head bare, bow in hand. And he ran for his life.

'He ran down an alleyway and ducked through an arch into a courtyard from where there was no escape other than the way he had entered. He had just realized his mistake when the arrow hit him and he dropped to the floor.

'I peeked out from behind a chimney to watch two men discover the body and declare him dead, baffled as to where his attacker had come from or gone to. I was about to make my escape, when I saw another man enter the courtyard. He talked to the men but was too far away for me to hear what he was saying. When the others were distracted, this third man leaned over the body, broke off the arrow flight and stuffed it into his pocket. Why would he do this? I wondered. I decided to follow him and it was not long before I saw his face; a face I had not seen in many years, but one I was not likely to forget.'

'Sergeant Quinn,' said Tom.

'Yes,' said Tonsahoten through gritted teeth. 'He walked through the city looking over his shoulder the whole time, as if a bear were at his heels.'

'Or a demon,' said Dr Harker. Tonsahoten looked puzzled. 'Please go on,' the doctor added.

'Will had planted all the cards, just as I had asked him to, but unknown to us, he had been discovered.'

'Discovered?' said Tom.

'Yes. Shepton must have seen him place a card in one of the other men's pockets and followed him. Sad to say, when I next appeared in front of Will, he ran from me in terror, having heard all about the Death and the Arrow murders. He feared me so much that he ran straight into the arms of Shepton.' The words were hard for Tom to hear and Dr Harker leaned over and put a hand on his shoulder.

'I was sorry for Will. Believe me. I saw you both at the funeral,' said the Mohawk.

'It was you,' said Tom. 'Standing in the street. It was you I saw.'

'Yes, it was me. I jumped aboard a passing cart before you could see me clearly.'

'And you followed us?' said Dr Harker.

'Yes,' said Tonsahoten. 'I heard you talk about the murders and about the sergeant. I saw the one called Ocean save you from two of the men I sought, while Shepton looked on from a safe distance. And I followed you to the Ten-killed Cat and found the sergeant. I waited nearby and took my chance, following a group of sailors down the stairs. I pulled my bow from under my coat and let loose an arrow as the sailors entered the room, hitting the sergeant before he even had a chance to pull the trigger of his pistol. Drink had dulled the wits of everyone there, and I was at the top of the stairs and out into the street before the bar maid screamed.'

'Have you no sorrow for taking another man's life?' said Dr Harker.

'None,' said the Mohawk solemnly. 'I would do it again, for all that he had done. My only sorrow is that Shepton still lives!'

18

THE CONDEMNED HOLD

Tonsahoten stood trial for murder at the Old Bailey at the next sessions. Leech's mother brought the prosecution. The place was packed, despite the rain bucketing down on them outside the Sessions House. The judge and jury sat under shelter, but the area for family, friends, enemies, witnesses, thief-catchers, journalists and other assorted courtroom hangers-on was open to the elements. The judges wanted to avoid close confinement with the stench and lice of the disease-ridden criminals – and the disease-ridden public.

Tom, Ocean and Dr Harker all attended, and Tom recognized several customers from The Quill. Under-marshal Hitchin was there too, smirking with satisfaction. And Tom noted with a special disgust that the sinister Dr Cornelius had also come to watch.

The outcome of the trial was never in doubt. The Mohawk remained silent throughout and did not react when the jury pronounced him guilty, or even when the judge condemned him to be hanged from the Tyburn gallows.

The crowd, on the other hand, cheered as if at a pantomime, delighted by the prospect of seeing this savage swing at the next Hanging Fair. They shouted and jeered and waved their hats, while Tonsahoten was taken back to Newgate.

Dr Harker led Ocean and Tom to The Quill

and the three of them sat in melancholy silence for some time. Eventually the doctor commented that though Tonsahoten was guilty of the murders and so by the law was justly condemned, he could see no evil in the man. Tom and Ocean agreed.

'I think he is a good man driven to bad deeds,' Dr Harker added.

'And he won't be the first of those to feel the noose,' said Ocean. 'Nor the last neither.'

Tom went to visit the Mohawk the following day. He dropped his money in the turnkey's filthy palm but the man blocked his way with his other arm. 'Another shilling if you wants to see the savage,' he said. His breath stank of gin and tobacco. 'He's very popular, that one. We likes our freaks, we do. Good for business.'

It was pointless to argue. Tom dug another shilling out of his pocket. It was just as well that Dr Harker had given him some money to take with him. Visiting Newgate was becoming an expensive business.

As Tom walked through into the Common

Ward, there was more of a commotion than usual. The door to the Condemned Hold stood wide open and, looking in, Tom saw that it was empty. Then he saw Tonsahoten, towering above a crowd of shouting inmates, turnkeys and assorted visitors. He pushed his way through the crowd and saw that in the centre of it was a cleared space, and in the centre of that was the Mohawk, chained hand and foot. He was stripped to the waist and Tom could see that the tattoos on his face continued down over his whole body.

The crowd had the look of madmen about them, as they yelled and jostled for a better position – gap-toothed mouths in wine-red faces bellowing and jabbering. The din was hellish. Only the Mohawk was calm.

'Come on, Foster, where's your man?' shouted one of the turnkeys. The crowd on the opposite side parted and an excited murmur ran round at the entry of another man, every bit as big as Tonsahoten and likewise stripped to the waist, likewise chained hand and foot. He had a gold ring in each ear and his head was smooth shaven.

Tom was beginning to realize what was going on.

'Come on, gentlemen,' cried the turnkey. 'Place your bets, place your bets. We have here a savage from the Americas up against this seafaring giant. Place your bets, gentlemen, on these fine gladiators. You'll not see a better fight than this in all of London!'

The two chained men looked at each other, both totally impassive, neither acknowledging the baying crowd around them. The men's size and bearing had the effect of making the others look like children.

'Very well, gentlemen,' said the turnkey. 'I won't trouble these two warriors with petty rules. Rules is for lords and earls and other like fops. So, when I drops my hand, one man will set about the other until one falls insensible to the floor. The man left standing at the end is the winner.'

The crowd pulled back to make room and to avoid becoming entangled in the fight. The turnkey dropped his hand and the sailor took a couple of steps towards the Mohawk, who continued to stare straight ahead.

The sailor looked suspiciously at Tonsahoten and then punched him on the side of the jaw. It was a blow that would have downed a horse, but the Mohawk shook his head and looked at the sailor. The sailor hit him again, but harder this time. Tonsahoten was forced to take a step back. The crowd grumbled. This was no kind of fight. The sailor looked about him and then squinted back at the Mohawk, trying to work out if this was some sort of ruse. 'Why won't you fight?' he asked. 'You can take a punch well enough. Are you a coward or a Quaker?'

'I have no argument with you,' said Tonsahoten calmly.

The sailor snorted and hit him again.

'They call you a seafaring man,' said Tonsahoten.

'What of it?' said the sailor, amazed that the Mohawk was still on his feet.

'I too know something of the sea.'

'I dare say you do,' said the sailor. 'I hardly thought you flew across the ocean.' The men round the sailor laughed. 'Now put up your hands, Indian, and fight like a man.' But

Tonsahoten did not move, and again the sailor hesitated.

'Come on!' shouted one of the men nearby. 'Get on with it! Kill him!'

'Put up your hands, savage,' said the sailor again.

'I will not,' said Tonsahoten. 'We are not chained bears to fight for their sport. We are free men.'

The sailor laughed. 'You don't look too free,' he said. 'And I don't feel it neither.'

'We are free men in chains,' said Tonsahoten. 'That is all. Look about you, mariner. Will a man like you fight on the say-so of men like these?' The sailor looked about him at the filthy, jeering crowd as if seeing them for the first time, then back at the Mohawk. 'Let us not shame ourselves for these bilge-rats,' Tonsahoten continued. 'We could have been shipmates once. Maybe we will still?'

The sailor smiled. 'Aye,' he said. 'Maybe we will at that. In any case, I'm not sure I could hit you any harder without breaking my fist.' He lowered his hands.

The crowd exploded with anger. Foster, the inmate who had brought the sailor to the fight, cursed and berated his protégé, until finally the big man cuffed him on the side of the head and he fell unconscious to the floor. 'Lord, how I miss the sea!' said the sailor, closing his eyes and shaking his head. 'Peace be with you, American,' he said, turning back to Tonsahoten.

'And with you,' replied the Mohawk.

'Come on, come on,' said the turnkey, jabbing Tonsahoten in the side with a pikestaff. 'If you ain't gonna fight, you can get back in the hold.' Other turnkeys dispersed the crowd.

As the Mohawk was being led back to the Condemned Hold, the Reverend Purney blocked his path. He had already tried several times to extract Tonsahoten's confession. It would make a bestseller – he was sure of it. 'I must have words with you, savage,' he said. 'Even though you are a heathen, you may yet save your soul, in the love of Our Lord Jesus Christ, if you repent of your sins and accept the one true God.'

'I have a god,' said Tonsahoten. 'I do not need another.'

'There is only one God,' said Purney. 'You must give up your heathen gods.'

'You take my land, and now you try to take my god?' said the Mohawk angrily.

Purney backed off nervously and tripped over, falling onto the pig, which squealed under his weight. The one-eyed dog lurched forward and made off with the reverend's wig in its jaws. Purney got to his feet as the whole room erupted in laughter, and ran off in pursuit of the dog.

The turnkey was still laughing as he pushed the Mohawk into the Condemned Hold. Tom ran over to the door just as the turnkey was locking it. 'I've come to see the Mohawk,' he said.

The turnkey shoved him away. 'No visitors,' he said.

'But—'

'*No visitors!*' yelled the turnkey, pointing the pikestaff at Tom.

Tom sighed and sadly made his way home.

Two days later Tom approached the prison once again in the hopes of seeing his friend. Just as he was joining the queue of visitors, a voice made him turn in panic.

'Well, well,' it said. 'If it isn't my young friend.' It was Shepton. Tom backed off towards the crowd.

'Don't worry,' said Shepton. 'I am not going to harm you – though I should, for what you did to Fisher. No, I am away to pastures new. Tell the savage that his actions have only served to make me even richer, for now all the remaining silver is mine, with none left to share it with. Thank him for me. Tell him that I wish I could see him hanged but I sail on tomorrow's tide.' With that he tipped his hat, grinned and walked away.

This time the turnkey would only let Tom whisper to the Mohawk through the grille of the door to the Condemned Hold. He could barely see Tonsahoten in the gloom, but when he told him about Shepton, he heard the links of his chains scrape together and a low groan like that of an injured bear.

The next morning, as Tom was trimming leaflets in the workshop with his father, the door burst open and Ocean almost fell in, panting for breath.

'Tom ... Mr Marlowe ... Begging your pardon ... It's—'

'What?' said Tom. 'Has something happened?'

'He ... He ... He's escaped!'

19

FROST FAIR

London buzzed like a beehive when it heard the news of the Mohawk's escape. He had broken free of his chains in the night and over-powered the turnkey who came to check on him. Wearing the turnkey's hat and wig, he had climbed the stairs leading onto the roof, leaped across to a nearby chimney stack and made off.

Ballads were sung and there was even a harlequinade called *The Cunning Savage* performed at the Drury Lane Theatre in Covent Garden, in which an actor with painted tattoos and holding a bow and arrow sang a song entitled, 'I was only a humble Savage, but now I'm the Talk of the Town.' Fashion-conscious fops took to wearing silk quivers over their shoulders filled with silver-tipped arrows with peacock-feather flights. Women wore the most ridiculous-looking feathered headdresses to the theatre and pinned bow and arrow brooches to their gowns.

The antics of the Mohocks had ceased to divert the newspaper-reading public. How could they compete with a real savage, a real Mohawk? True, young rakes tried their hands at archery until a handful of ugly accidents forced the city to ban bows and arrows completely. But in any case London soon became bored with Indians and arrows and the like.

Tom was glad that Tonsahoten had got away;

he was relieved to see his hanging day come and go, with the hangman cheated. Dr Harker too seemed happy with how things had turned out. Ocean drank the Mohawk's health and wished him well. All three hoped he would return to his life at sea and forget about Shepton.

A friend of Ocean's had confirmed that Shepton had indeed left London, buying passage for himself on a ship bound for Alexandria. He had evaded justice for Will's murder, but Tom was just glad that he was now half a world away.

And so, gradually, Tom's life returned to its old pattern, though there was one welcome change. Ocean began working in the print shop. The Lamb and Lion had never been busier and Tom and his father welcomed the extra set of hands. For his part Ocean was grateful for the trust they put in him.

The summer of 1715 was hardly any summer at all. Tom braved rainstorm after rainstorm to see to it that there were always fresh flowers on Will's grave. The city streets were filled with filthy puddles and the gutters became small rivers, carrying their stinking flotsam downstream to the Fleet ditch and that sewer of all sewers, the Thames itself.

Winter, when it came, was as sharp as an axe. A bitter wind gnawed at the city and those who could afford it piled the hearth high with sea coal, fresh off the colliers down from the Tyne. Those who could not afford it did the best they could, or died. The smoke from the sea coal blackened the London sky even more. And not just the sky: the houses, the shops, even the horses and the good people of London themselves were covered in the soot that fell from the foul-smelling smog.

Ice formed on the rancid waters of the Fleet ditch as snow fell on the dome of St Paul's. Horses fought to keep their footing on the frozen cobbles and Londoners slipped and slid their way from home to coffee house, from market place to theatre. Slowly, as the nights grew ever colder, ice began to spread out from the banks of the Thames, blue-grey above the waters of the river. Watermen found it harder to get from shore to shore. Even the rushing weir between the arches of London Bridge slowly turned to ice. The river was frozen over.

The watermen were furious, their livelihood gone. What use was a ferryman now that a person could walk from Charing Cross to Southwark? But for Tom, and most of the rest of London, the freezing of the Thames was a cause for celebration, because it meant there could be a Frost Fair!

Tom came on the first night to help his father set up a stall selling commemorative posters and prints. It was an amazing sight. Striped tents crowded the ice, with multi-coloured flags and bunting flapping in the breeze. There was a man juggling flaming torches, a woman walking a tightrope; there were beer tents and pie-stalls, puppet shows and music; goldsmiths and silversmiths hammered away. People of every kind and class, dressed in silk or dressed in rags, all marvelled at the scene.

The prints on Mr Marlowe's stall were selling like hot cakes. Ocean had also agreed to help Tom's father and proved to be a natural sales-man. In fact he was doing so well that Mr

Marlowe had to ask Tom to return to the print shop and collect some more stock.

Tom was reluctant to tear himself away from the fair, but Fleet Street was not far away. He would be back in no time. He set off across the ice and up some steps leading to the Strand. He was almost at the top when someone grabbed him from behind.

'Where is he, boy?' hissed his attacker.

'Who? What do you want? I have no money—'

'The savage. The Mohawk. Where is he?' As the man asked the question, he spun Tom round and showed his scarred and evil face.

'Shepton!' said Tom.

'You have not forgotten me then?' said Shepton. 'Or what I am?'

'No!' shouted Tom. 'You are a murderer!'

'Then know that I will not hesitate to end your puny life if you do not straightaway tell me of the whereabouts of that savage.'

'I don't know,' said Tom. 'How could I? He is long gone.'

'Gone from you, maybe,' said Shepton, 'but

not from me. I have travelled the world, and everywhere I turn he follows me, like some sort of devil. Wherever I go, among Turks or Spaniards, Chinamen or Arabs, there he is. He has dogged my every step these past months, trailing me around the globe.' His face contorted into a sneer. 'But as you see, he has not done for me, for all his efforts, and I will kill him yet. Where is he, boy?'

'I swear that I do not know,' said Tom.

'Then you are of no use to me, are you, boy. Farewell.' Shepton put his hands to Tom's throat and began to squeeze. Tom's struggles were of no use and quickly began to fade.

'Leave the boy alone!'

Shepton loosened his grip on Tom, who collapsed to the ground, and turned to see who had shouted. He let out a contemptuous laugh as he saw Dr Harker standing a few yards distant. 'You?' he shouted. 'You dare to challenge me?'

'I have a sword!'

Shepton laughed again and, pulling his own sword from its scabbard, walked towards the doctor. 'Then draw it and use it!' he said.

20

BLOOD ON THE ICE

Tom shouted, 'No!' as Shepton swept back his arm and slashed his sword straight at Dr Harker's head. But to the surprise of both Tom and Shepton the doctor effortlessly parried the blow and sent his attacker stumbling across the steps.

Shepton squinted at him, trying to determine whether or not it had been a lucky move. He recovered his balance and this time lunged at Dr Harker with the point of his sword aimed at the doctor's stomach, but again his opponent easily avoided it, scooping up and diverting the attack. Again Shepton thrust and this time Dr Harker merely sidestepped the blow. Shepton tried to bring his sword down on top of the doctor's head, but Dr Harker swung his own sword to meet it, pulled it round in a flashing arc and sent it clattering across the steps, with Shepton bolting after it.

Shepton picked up the sword, yelled in frustration and ran at the doctor, hacking alternately at each shoulder, but Dr Harker was too quick for him, blocking each blow effortlessly. Shepton struck again and again – so quickly that Tom could follow the strokes only by the sparks that flew as the swords met – but each time Dr Harker parried the blows, finally striking a blow himself that cut through Shepton's coat and on into enough flesh to make him wince.

Shepton backed off to a safe distance and let

his sword arm drop. He put his hand to the wound to his shoulder and felt the blood that had begun to leak through the cut cloth. He looked at Dr Harker with a smile that, on a face less evil, might have passed for one of admiration. 'I've misjudged you, sir,' he said, putting away his sword and pulling out a pistol. 'Drop it!' Dr Harker dropped the sword, which clattered across the stone steps. 'Now,' Shepton went on, 'let's see if you die as well as you fence.'

Just then Tom saw something on the roof. A black shape on the roof ridge. A glint of metal.

Shepton saw Tom look, turned and dived to his right as the arrow hit the steps. He fired his pistol wildly in the direction of the shot. 'Come on, you devil!' he shouted, scrabbling to his feet and seeking the cover of a low wall. 'Show your face!' He turned and walked towards Dr Harker with the now empty pistol, and without warning struck the doctor on the side of the head with it.

'Dr Harker!' shouted Tom, as the doctor dropped to the floor.

Shepton put the empty pistol in his belt and pulled out another. 'This one is loaded, count on that,' he said as he put it to Tom's ribs and dragged him down the steps, back towards the frozen river and the fair.

Ocean saw them as they came onto the ice and vaulted the table to follow them. Then Dr Harker staggered towards him, and Tom's father came across to see what was going on.

'No, Ocean,' warned the doctor. 'Shepton has a pistol. He'll kill Tom for sure if we try to stop him.'

'But we must do *something*!' shouted Mr Marlowe.

'We can only follow and see what chance we may have to free Tom,' said Dr Harker.

'Quickly then,' said Ocean.

The three men pushed their way through the crowd, looking around for any sign of Shepton and Tom, three grim faces in a sea of laughing and singing ones. A jig rang out from the beer tent as Ocean spotted Shepton heading towards London Bridge. He tapped his two friends and pointed.

The crowd thinned as Tom and Shepton approached the bridge. Tom could feel the barrel of the flintlock pistol pressed hard against his side, as Shepton shoved and tugged him along. He was about to ask where his captor was taking him, when they halted under one of the arches, which was thick with icicles. Shepton turned back towards the fair.

Tom immediately saw his father, Dr Harker and Ocean. They had stopped in a row about fifty yards away. Tom's father was about to shout out when Shepton beat him to it.

'Savage!' he shouted. 'Show yourself, you devil! You've stalked me long enough, you filthy coward. Face me like a man, if you call yourself a man!'

Shepton took the pistol from Tom's ribs, pointed it in the air and pulled the trigger. The boom of the blast shook the icicles above their heads and Tom heard them creak and crack. It also brought a crowd from the fair, eager for more entertainment.

Shepton threw the pistol to the ground. 'No guns, no arrows!' he shouted, as he pulled a large knife from his belt. The crowd gasped and Tom's father stepped forward, but Shepton put the knife to Tom's throat. 'Not one step further.'

'Let the boy go!' The Mohawk pushed his way to the front of the crowd, and between Dr Harker and Mr Marlowe.

Shepton pushed the boy away. 'Drop that cursed bow!'

The Mohawk took the bow from his shoulder and passed it to Ocean, and did the same with the quiver of arrows. 'Here is where it ends,' said Tonsahoten quietly. He took off his hat, his wig and his coat and stood in his beaded jacket. Around his neck was a knife in a leather sheath. He drew it and the blade sparkled in the torchlight.

'Well, come on, savage!' shouted Shepton. 'Or have you not the stomach for a real fight?'

Tonsahoten lowered his head and began to run towards his enemy, but Tom noticed Shepton reach into his pocket and produce yet another pistol. Tom jumped to his feet as Shepton took aim and rushed at him, pushing up his arm as he pulled the trigger. But the shot still hit the Mohawk and he dropped to the ice.

Shepton shoved Tom away and yelled out in triumph as he saw the Mohawk's still form. He pulled out a bent and dog-eared Death and the Arrow card from his pocket and waved it at the hushed crowd. 'Do you see?' he shouted wildly arching backwards, arms outstretched. 'Do you see? I have beaten this card and I have beaten Death!'

At that moment Tom heard another cracking noise from the arch above and both he and Shepton looked up at the sound. Tom cried out as half a dozen icicles hurtled down, two of them jabbing into the ice inches away from him.

When he looked at Shepton, his captor was still looking up, his back to the crowd. He rocked slightly from toe to heel, then fell backwards with six inches of a foot-long icicle sticking out from his chest. The Death and the Arrow card dropped from his fingers and fluttered away across the ice.

Mr Marlowe rushed to embrace his son. 'Tom, Tom,' he said with tears in his eyes. 'I thought I'd lost you for good, there, lad.'

'The Mohawk, Father,' said Tom. 'Tonsahoten . . . Is he . . .?'

'Dr Harker is with him, son.'

Tom ran over to the fallen Mohawk but Ocean

blocked his path. 'Leave him be, Tom. You cannot help him now.'

Tom looked past Ocean's outstretched arm and saw Dr Harker leaning over the body. He turned to Tom and shook his head. Tom pushed Ocean away and strode off across the ice alone. His father called him back but he paid no heed.

It was fifteen minutes before he wandered back again, a little ashamed at himself, having rehearsed an apology to all concerned. He pushed through the crowd to find a black wagon pulled by two black horses leaving the scene. Under-marshal Hitchin and his men were dispersing the crowd and Hitchin tipped his hat at Tom and smiled. The bodies of both the Mohawk and Shepton were gone. Only two bloodstains on the ice remained.

'Sorry,' said Tom, as he found his father and friends.

'There's no need,' said his father.

'But what was that wagon?' said Tom.

'You remember Dr Cornelius . . .?' said Dr Harker.

Tom took a half step backwards, staring from

face to face. 'You have given the Mohawk to surgeons?' he yelled at the doctor. 'You gave him to those vultures!'

'But Tom—' began Dr Harker.

'Don't talk to me!' shouted Tom, waving him away and walking towards the shore. 'Not now, not ever!'

Tom to talk to me. Lord John was not happy about it and that annoys me. I shan't go now.

21

A NEW CUSTOMER

Tom refused to talk about Dr Harker, though his father tried several times over the next few days when they were working together in the print shop. Ocean, too, tried his best to broach the subject, but Tom would have none of it.

Ocean was working full time at the Lamb and Lion now. Tom's father seemed to have taken quite a shine to him, despite his life of thievery, possibly to make amends for his behaviour towards Will Piggot.

Tom tried his best to forget about Dr Harker and the worlds he had opened up to him, though he missed him and he missed their talks. But the doctor had betrayed him. He knew Tom's feelings about the surgeons, and yet he had paid no heed.

Then one morning Mr Marlowe turned to Ocean and told him that he needed some pamphlets delivering to an address in Mayfair. 'It's a new customer; they sent a messenger round yesterday morning. I don't like working for people I have never met, so make sure you get paid.' Ocean could deliver them, he said, but he wanted Tom to go with him to keep him company. 'It's not that I don't trust you, mind. But these things have to be done right, and Tom has been delivering for me for many years now and never lost me a customer.'

'That's understood, Mr Marlowe,' said Ocean. 'Shall we go, Tom?'

Tom washed his hands and put on his coat, and they each picked up a parcel of pamphlets, wrapped in brown paper, tied with string and stamped with an image of the Lamb and Lion.

'Here's the address, Ocean,' said Mr Marlowe, handing him a piece of paper. 'They're expecting you.'

Tom and Ocean set off for Mayfair. The Great Frost was thawing and sleet was falling on the coffee-coloured slush of the city streets. They walked through the arch of Temple Bar and onto the Strand, past the pillory where an old man sobbed, his face cut and bruised, and laughing workhouse children clutched stones in their grubby hands. They walked through Covent Garden and Leicester Fields.

'He's a good man, your father,' commented Ocean as the snow began to fall more steadily.

'I know it,' said Tom.

'Not many would give work to such as me. I shan't let him down.'

'I know that too,' said Tom with a smile. 'But where is this place? My boots are soaked through.'

'Not far now,' said Ocean. 'It's the next on the left.'

They turned into a street that was lined with fine houses. Ocean consulted the piece of paper Mr Marlowe had given him and then pointed to a house nearby. 'That's our boy,' he said.

The door was opened by a manservant who, when they told him they had a delivery from the Lamb and Lion print shop, said that his master had asked that they come in. He wanted to take possession of the pamphlets personally.

Tom and Ocean took off their hats, shook their wet coats and were led into the hall. The servant said that he would only be a moment and disappeared through a door to fetch his master. The hall was very grand. There were gold-framed paintings on the wall and a large clock ticked away in the corner. At the foot of the staircase was a mahogany table on which were two huge silver candlesticks and a large leather-bound book. Tom could see something peeping out from under the book and, out of curiosity, lifted the book to see what it was. He could hardly believe his eyes. It was a Death and the Arrow card.

'Master will see you now,' said a voice behind him.

Tom backed towards the front door. 'And who is your master?' he asked as a man came into view walking slowly down the stairs.

'It is I,' said the man. 'Dr Cornelius.'

'You!' shouted Tom. 'What kind of joke is this?'

'There is no joke, I assure you, Master Marlowe,' said Dr Cornelius. 'I have something I wish to show you.'

'There is nothing you could show me that I would want to see! Come on, Ocean. Let's leave the pamphlets and quit this place.' Tom banged his parcel violently down on the table – so violently that the brown paper split and he could see the contents. 'What is this?' he muttered, ripping the paper aside. Inside were sheaves of blank paper.

'Forgive the ruse, Tom.' It was Dr Harker, who had suddenly appeared behind Dr Cornelius.

Tom was furious and turned on Ocean. 'You knew about this?' he asked indignantly.

'I did. And your father too,' said Ocean.

'I thought you were my friend,' he said to Ocean, tears welling in his eyes.

'That I am,' said Ocean, grabbing both Tom's shoulders.

Tom shrugged him away. 'And yet you trick me into coming to this house, of all houses, just to see Dr Harker—'

'Not *just* to see me,' said Dr Harker.

A door opened behind the doctor and Tom stepped back in amazement as Tonsahoten emerged.

'But you're—'

'Dead?' asked the Mohawk. 'No, I am as alive as you.'

Tom looked around in bafflement. Everyone laughed.

'Well, are you not pleased to see me living?' asked Tonsahoten with a grin.

'Yes . . . Yes . . . More than I can say.'

The Mohawk gripped him in a bear hug, wincing slightly as he did so.

'Will someone tell me what is happening?' asked Tom.

'I'm sorry, Tom,' said Dr Harker. 'There had to

be secrecy in this. Ocean and your father knew nothing until this morning and Ocean wanted to keep the good news as a surprise until you got here. Tonsahoten is a condemned felon. If Hitchin's men had known he was alive, they would have taken him to be hanged.'

'But I thought you had been shot,' said Tom to the Mohawk.

'I was, Tom,' said Tonsahoten. 'But your efforts meant that Shepton missed my heart. Dr Cornelius pulled the shot from my shoulder. He has great skill, Tom.'

Dr Cornelius blushed. 'The ice stopped the bleeding,' he explained, 'and slowed his heart and breathing enough to fool that jackal Hitchin and his men. In fact, Dr Harker did well to realize this man was alive at all; a weaker man might have died in any case. The doctor sent for me as soon as he could and I did my best – he had already told me of the wrongs the Mohawk had suffered, and I hoped to make amends in some small way.'

'I was wrong about you,' said Tom, shaking the doctor's hand. 'I'm sorry for it. You saved Tonsahoten's life.'

'And put his own at risk,' said Ocean. 'Helping a convicted felon is a hanging crime. We could all swing if this ever got out.'

'Which is why I must leave on the next tide,' said the Mohawk. 'I have put you all in enough danger. There is no homeland for me now, so I will return to the only other place I have known happiness – to the sea, to a life of roving. But I shall not forget you.'

'Nor I you,' said Tom.

'Nor any of us,' said Dr Harker.

Tom, Ocean and Dr Harker took Tonsahoten down to the quay that very night. There was no moon and the back streets they walked were as dark as tunnels. Tom was nervous even with the Mohawk, Ocean and Dr Harker's sword arm beside him.

They walked in silence, each of them with much that they would have liked to say, but aware that there was no time. There was still danger in their expedition. Until Tonsahoten was safely aboard the ship, Tyburn's gallows loomed large – and for all of them now, for the help they had given to an escaped felon.

They had just reached the foot of a long flight of steps when they heard the sound of running feet. Quiet at first, the noise became louder and louder and wild voices could be heard above it. The four friends turned to see a group of young men rushing towards them, howling like banshees.

The leading member of the gang signalled for the others to stop and he himself came to a halt a yard or two in front of Tom and the others. His face might have been handsome once, but was now deathly pale. His eyes glinted like glass beads. He had fine lace at his throat and wrists and spoke in loud, nasal tones, toying absent-mindedly with an enormous clasp knife. Tom felt himself shuffling backwards.

'I feel duty bound to inform you,' said the man with all the solemnity of a Justice of the Peace, 'that you have had the grave misfortune to cross paths with the most bloodthirsty coven of cut-throats ever to tread these streets.' He made a theatrical bow and then gestured towards the rest of the gang. 'You may have heard tell of the

Mohocks!' he said, and the others resumed their howling.

Tom looked at Dr Harker, Dr Harker at Ocean, Ocean at Tonsahoten and then back along the line until Ocean said, 'Enough of this foppish nonsense!' All at once, he pulled a pistol from each coat pocket and Dr Harker drew his sword, and all three weapons aimed at the startled Mohock's head. His knife slipped from his fingers and fell to the ground. His colleagues began to melt away into the darkness.

'You may also have heard tell of me,' said Tonsahoten. He had removed his hat and wig and carried his bow raised and ready; he walked forward until the tip of his arrow rested on the young man's nose, making a tiny dent in the pale flesh. Terrified, the Mohock turned on his heels and ran, stumbling as he went, losing a shoe but lacking the nerve to retrieve it.

'Shall we continue on our way?' said Dr Harker after they had managed to stop laughing.

'We'd better, if our friend's going to catch his ride,' said Ocean.

'You scared the life out of that Mohock,' said Tom.

'And it ain't going to get any better for him neither,' said Ocean, slapping Tom on the back. 'I slipped a Death and the Arrow card into his pocket.' Everyone laughed at the thought of that – even Tonsahoten.

But the laughter faded, for in no time at all they were standing on the quayside, listening to the mysterious clamour of sailors going about their given tasks – busy silhouettes among the rigging, knotting and loosening ropes, hauling in chains and unfurling canvas.

The ice on the river had melted and ships were free to sail once more. Tonsahoten stood beside the gangplank of his ship, a brig called the *Dolphin*, bound for the West Indies. He embraced each of the friends in turn, then took a necklace from around his throat and gave it to Tom. It was a thin strip of leather threaded through with a small white shell. 'Farewell, Tom,' he said.

'Farewell,' said Tom in return, and before he had put the necklace over his head, Tonsahoten was stepping aboard the ship.

All too soon they were ready to sail, the mooring ropes were loosed and the tide took the *Dolphin* away downriver towards the sea and the rest of the world. Tom stood and waved, waiting and watching until they could see nothing but the bare horizon and the new day dawning.

As they walked away from the river, Dr Harker put his arm round Tom's shoulder. 'Tom, lad,' he said, 'I wondered how you might feel about becoming my assistant?' Tom stopped in his tracks. 'It's high time I sorted my books and my collection of curiosities; and I can think of no one I'd rather have to help me do it. I've neglected things lately, but these last months have given me a new lease of life. Who knows, I may even go voyaging again – with you at my side, if you're willing. What do you say?'

Tom's face lit up and then just as quickly fell. 'I would love to, Dr Harker,' he said. 'But I cannot. As I have told you, my father needs me in the printing house. I cannot desert him.'

'I have already spoken to your father and he has given his consent,' said the doctor. 'He has taken on an apprentice of his own.'

'He has?' said Tom, surprised that his father had not mentioned it to him.

'Yes, Tom,' said Ocean. 'Me!' Tom looked amazed. 'What's this?' laughed Ocean. 'You don't think I'd make a worthy apprentice? I'm hurt! Sore hurt!'

Tom laughed and clapped him on the shoulder. 'I can think of none better,' he said and turned to Dr Harker with a grin. 'Well, then, I shall be proud to be your assistant, Doctor.'

'Splendid,' said Dr Harker. 'It has been quite an adventure, has it not? I think that it might make a diverting story, written down well. I will have a word with your father this very day about the possibility of publishing a small book. Now, who's for coffee?'

If you enjoyed *Death and the Arrow*, you'll love the next Tom Marlowe adventure, when Tom and Dr Harker investigate the mystery of the White Rider, a masked highwayman who is rumoured to be able to kill his victims just by pointing at them!

Turn over to read the first two chapters of *The White Rider* . . .

1

TOWER HILL

Achill breeze blew from east of the City, carrying on its breath the rancid taint of glue works and tanners' yards. It filled the sails of merchantmen and barges and shivered the surface of the Thames. It twisted the weather vanes on the turrets of the Tower of London and ruffled the black drapes on the scaffold on Tower Hill.

Grim-faced soldiers gripped their pikes and sword hilts while the crowd shifted their feet and blew on their hands to ward off the cold. There was a general muttering and grumbling about the wait, and the occasional chuckle and guffaw about the news that Lord Nithsdale had escaped from the Tower the day before dressed as a woman.

And in among the crowd was Tom Marlowe, fifteen years old – though he was soon to be sixteen – and the assistant of the man who stood at his side: the brilliant Dr Josiah Harker. Dr Harker had given no explanation why he wanted them to come to Tower Hill, but Tom had been through so much with the doctor in recent months that he would have followed him into a burning house without question.

A murmur ran through the onlookers as the Earl of Derwentwater finally mounted the scaffold. Tom wondered at how calm he looked, and his voice sounded clear when he turned to the crowd and spoke. After saying a few prayers, Derwentwater retracted his guilty plea and spoke warmly in praise of the exiled son of James II: James Francis Edward Stuart, the man he believed should rightfully be sitting on the throne now occupied by George I.

Tom listened as Derwentwater told the crowd that there would never be peace in the country until the Stuarts were restored to the throne, but few in England would have shared that view. They wanted no more papists on the throne.

The new King George may have been German, but he was a Protestant. Better a foreigner than a Catholic. There would be no James III despite all the efforts of his supporters, the Jacobites.

'I die a Roman Catholic,' said Derwentwater. 'I am in perfect charity with all the world – I thank God for it – even with those of the present government, who are the most instrumental in my death.'

There were more murmurs, though Tom could not tell whether they were murmurs against Derwentwater or against the government.

'I freely forgive such ungenerously reported

false things of me,' continued Derwentwater. 'And I hope to be forgiven the trespasses of my youth, by the Father of infinite mercy, into whose hands I commend my soul.'

He handed the paper on which his speech had been written to the sheriff and looked at the wooden block in front of him. Laughter rippled through the crowd as he asked the axeman to chip off a splinter of wood in case he hurt his neck. Then Derwentwater took off his coat and his waistcoat and kneeled down. A hush fell as he laid his head on the block.

'Lord Jesu receive my soul,' he prayed as the axe was raised. 'Lord Jesu receive my soul. Lord Jesu receive my soul—'

The axe fell and Tom shut his eyes and wished he could have shut his ears to the noise of the axe's striking. But when he opened his eyes there was even more horror and he turned away from the sight, but not before he had caught a glimpse of the axeman holding Derwentwater's head aloft for the crowd to see.

'Behold the head of a traitor!' he shouted. 'God save King George!'

The crowd erupted into cheering and booing, but again, Tom found it impossible to tell whether they were cheering Derwentwater or the king, or booing a traitor or the government that killed him.

The body was wrapped in black and taken away and then Lord Kenmure appeared. Tom thought how much harder it must be to come to the scaffold when it was already damp with blood. Kenmure had pleaded for mercy at his trial; but he stood bravely now, though he made no speech. He prayed, said a couple of words to the axeman and kneeled before the block.

This time Tom turned away and watched Dr Harker's face. He heard the axe come down once, then again. The doctor did not flinch either time, but looked straight ahead, even when the executioner once more said the words, 'Behold the head of a traitor,' and Tom knew what his friend must be seeing. Still he stared fixedly while the cheering and jeering broke out once more. His gaze did not waver, even when the crowd, encouraged by the soldiers, began to move away and disperse. Tom had to tug hard on the doctor's arm before his trance was broken, and when he turned to Tom he had tears in his eyes. He closed them and shook his head.

'I should not have brought you here, Tom,' he said. 'You should not have seen this. I am sorry, truly I am.'

'Why were you so determined that we came?' asked Tom.

'Well, Tom, I wanted—' began the doctor, but he was interrupted by a man standing behind him.

'Josiah Harker, as I live and breathe,' he said, clapping a hand on Dr Harker's shoulder.

'Who the devil . . . ? I don't believe it! Daniel . . . Well, how are you, man?'

The two men embraced like long-lost brothers, slapping each other's shoulders and laughing like schoolboys. It seemed a long time before Dr Harker remembered that Tom was with him.

'Daniel, Daniel,' he said, slightly out of breath. 'You must meet my very able assistant and good friend Thomas Marlowe. Tom, this is a very old friend of mine, Daniel Thornley.'

'I am delighted to make your acquaintance,

Tom,' said Thornley, shaking Tom by the hand.

'And I yours,' said Tom.

Thornley was tall, and though he was probably a similar age to Dr Harker, he was leaner and fitter. He had a huge bright smile, his cheeks pulling back in curved creases to accommodate it. He had a relaxed air about him that put Tom immediately at ease, but his clothes were cheap and ill fitting, at odds with his voice and his bearing.

'What brings you here, Josiah?' asked Thornley, nodding his head towards the scaffold that was already being stripped of its black drapes.

'I might ask the same thing,' said Dr Harker.

'I have a professional interest in these matters, as you know, Josiah.'

'Yes, of course.' Dr Harker's smile faded a little. 'I suppose I had hoped you might have changed trades.'

Thornley smiled and then narrowed his eyes as he seemed to catch sight of something over Tom's shoulder. Tom followed his gaze but saw nothing but the remnants of the dispersing crowd.

'Let us not rekindle this old debate, Josiah,' said Thornley. 'I must go now, in any case. Shall we meet again? Do you still frequent The Quill coffee house?'

'Yes, I do,' said Dr Harker. 'But how do you know—?'

'Splendid, splendid. Then I shall see you in there very soon, Josiah. Very nice to meet you, Tom.'

Thornley walked off into the crowd and, with what seemed to Tom an almost supernatural ease, disappeared into it.

2

MONSIEUR PETIT

A golden haze lay across London like a silk
scarf, softening the shapes of buildings,
muting the colours. It conjured up something
beautiful and dreamlike out of the cold, damp
morning. Even the usual forge-like clatter and

clang of the city seemed to have stilled itself in sympathy with the scene.

Frost silvered the grass of St Bride's church-yard, twinkling as it began to melt, and made the shadows in the carvings on the gravestones shimmer blue. Cobwebs glistened, strung with pearl-like beads of water. The wrought-iron gate creaked at Tom's touch.

He left the slippery flagstone path leading to the church, walked across the wet grass and stopped in front of a headstone. The stone looked fresh save for a light coating of London grime; a year had not much weathered it and the carving was still as sharp as the day it was chiselled. A blackbird landed on a nearby railing, its tail rising as it rocked first forwards then back. It opened its yellow beak and sang out loud and long, its throat quivering, its wings twitching. Then it flew off, chattering away into the distance. Silence returned.

HERE LIES THE BODY OF WILL PIGGOT. Tom still found it hard to read the words, and even in the reading of them he found it harder still to accept that his friend really did lie beneath his feet and that he would never again see his face or hear his voice. It was hard to bear and Tom closed his eyes and hung his head.

'Here I am, Will,' said Tom without looking up. 'Here to show I haven't forgotten you. Nor ever will.' He opened his eyes and looked at the headstone once more.

On these visits to Will's grave, Tom increasingly found himself talking to the slightly startled-looking cherub that was carved into the top of the headstone above a scroll with REST IN PEACE written across it. It made him smile. Will could not have been farther from a cherub in life, and yet . . . and yet, there was something of Will in that carved cherub: the crooked smile, the long jaw and the deer-like alertness that had served him so well. Until the day of his murder, that is.

Will's friendship and, more especially, his untimely death, had changed Tom Marlowe's life for ever. Though Tom would have given anything to have Will standing there with him again, the tragedy had set Tom on an adventure that had made his life a thousand times richer than before. It was something that made him feel more than a little guilty: that he should have gained in any way from poor Will's terrible death.

If Will had not been murdered he would probably still be apprenticed to his father at the Lamb and Lion printing house, and he would certainly never have met the amazing Ocean Carter. Will had been Ocean's friend too, and Ocean had joined forces with Tom and Dr Harker to track down his killer. He was like no one Tom had ever met before; a cat-like visitor from London's underworld, quick-witted and fearless.

And now Ocean worked for Tom's father in his place and Tom worked for Dr Harker, cataloguing the doctor's enormous collection of artefacts collected on his travels and adventures around the world, living in an attic room at the top of his house in Fleet Street.

'You used to love to hear about Dr Harker's travels, didn't you, Will?' said Tom. 'You'd have loved to see all the things we've been cataloguing. We used to talk about how we'd run away to sea one day, didn't we? We used to say we'd go to America and seek our fortunes. I wonder if we ever would have done?'

Tom sat down on the cold stone tomb nearby, looked at the cherub smiling back at him and closed his eyes against the tears.

'Morning, Tom,' said Ocean as Tom walked into the printing house. He wiped as much ink from his hand as he could and offered it to Tom, who shook it warmly, slapping him on the arm.

'How are you, Ocean?' Tom asked. 'Father still keeping you busy?'

'I should say so, Tom,' he replied. 'It's all right for you, sitting around all day looking at books and the like. Some of us have real work to do.'

'I've done my share of work in this place,' said Tom, patting one of the presses warmly. 'I miss it sometimes, though. Is he about? Dr Harker's fussing about his books.'

'He's in the shop, Tom,' said Ocean. 'He'll be glad to see you.'

Tom walked through the door and found Mr Marlowe sitting deep in concentration, surrounded by piles of prints.

'Tom!' Mr Marlowe looked up from a print he was reading. 'Just reading this sermon about how

219

we are all about to be consumed by hell fire. "The Day of Judgement is upon us ... These are the Last Days." I can't think how many of these I've printed in my life; yet here we all are.' He chuckled to himself as he got up and clapped his huge hands on Tom's shoulders. 'It's good to see you, son.'

'And you, Father,' said Tom. 'Dr Harker wondered if his books were back from the binders yet.'

'Not yet, no. Tell him they'll be done by Friday.'

'I will, Father,' said Tom, dropping his voice to a conspiratorial whisper. 'How's Ocean getting on?'

'He's a godsend, to be honest, Tom,' said Mr Marlowe. 'You'd think he'd been in the business all his life. He's a deep one, though. A bit like you in that respect.'

Tom returned Mr Marlowe's smile. 'I do believe you're growing fond of Ocean, Father.'

'I am,' said Mr Marlowe, as if the thought had only that instant entered his head. 'I believe I am.' He blushed slightly at the realization that not so long ago he would never have countenanced even employing a man of Ocean's shady background. He had disapproved of Tom's friendship with Will Piggot, and taking Ocean on had been a kind of penance after Will's murder. But now he found that he simply liked having Ocean around, and it helped sweeten the loss of Tom to Dr Harker. 'And by the way,' he went on. 'What's this I hear about Dr Harker taking you to Tower Hill, Tom?'

'To the execution, yes,' said Tom. 'It was horrible, Father.'

'I can't say that I approve, Tom,' said Mr Marlowe. 'I don't have any great sympathy for those Jacobite traitors, but even so . . . It's a grim piece of entertainment for a lad of your age. Why did Harker feel the need to go?'

'I'm not altogether sure,' Tom replied. 'He said we would be witnessing history, but I'm not sure there wasn't more to it than that.'

'These Jacobite rascals are everywhere, Tom. Mr Finch was in yesterday – you know, the baker on Goat Lane whose brother is a turnkey in Newgate? He says that London is crawling with them. He says that people think they're all Scottish, but they have scores of sympathizers in

England . . . and in this very city. Think of that, Tom: in this very city. He says you can't tell who they might be, neither. It might be someone you've known for years. They'll get more than they bargained for if they come here, I'll tell you that for nothing.' Mr Marlowe picked up a hammer and weighed it in his hand. 'You can't trust anyone, that's what Finch says. You can't trust anyone. That's what the world's come to, Tom. It's all good for business though, I have to say. The printing house has never been busier, with all the pamphlets and sermons being churned out.'

'You don't think that . . .' began Tom and then shook his head.

'What is it, Tom?'

'You don't think it possible that Dr Harker might be a Jacobite sympathizer, do you?'

'Dr Harker!' said Mr Marlowe with a laugh. 'Never!' But then he saw the serious look on Tom's face and furrowed his brow. 'Why would you think such a thing?'

'It's just that . . . it's just a feeling I have about

the execution. There was something more to it than Dr Harker was saying.'

'Come on, Tom,' said Mr Marlowe. 'After all you've been through with Dr Harker, you can't believe he would lie to you? He doesn't seem the type for secrets. He probably just thought seeing an execution would be educational. You can't get everything out of books.'

When Tom turned the corner into the courtyard of Dr Harker's house, he took out his watch and remembered that the doctor had said that he had some business and would be out until ten o'clock. However, the maid, Sarah, would let him in and Tom was more than happy to while away the time in Dr Harker's study.

To his surprise, though, when Sarah opened the door she said she was sure the doctor was in because she had heard him walking about as she cleaned. So Tom climbed the stairs to the study. Above him, he heard raised voices: one was Dr Harker's, but the other he did not recognize. He was about to lay his hand on the brass doorknob of the study, when he paused.

The door was very slightly ajar and Tom could just see Dr Harker. He was talking to another man who was seated with his back to Tom. As Tom peered into the room, the man handed something to the doctor. Tom could not see what it was, save that it glinted as it caught the light from the nearby window. Dr Harker studied it and then put it in his waistcoat pocket. Tom knocked at the door and walked in. The stranger jumped up and reached into his pocket. Dr Harker grabbed his arm.

'Tom!' said the doctor with a rather forced laugh. 'Come in, come in. I would like you to meet my friend, Monsieur . . . Petit.'

The two men exchanged a furtive glance and then the stranger smiled and held out a hand. '*Bonjour*, Tom,' he said, with a thick French accent. 'I am very pleased to meet you.'

The man was tall and broad shouldered. Although the clothes he wore were stylish – verging on the foppish even – and obviously expensive, his appearance was a little dishevelled. As he took Tom's hand Tom noticed that his lace cuff was frayed and grubby.

He seemed an unlikely friend for Dr Harker.

Monsieur Petit's broad and handsome face was unshaven, the bristles, like his eyebrows, fair, and though his smile was warm enough, his clear grey eyes studied Tom with a wolf-like intensity. Tom was forced to look away and turned to Dr Harker.

'Monsieur . . . Petit is in London for a few days on business,' said the doctor, once again exchanging a glance with his guest that Tom felt he was not supposed to see. 'He is in the silk trade, with family in Spitalfields.' Tom thought that a man in the silk trade ought to have cleaner cuffs. 'He was just leaving.'

The stranger bowed and shook Dr Harker's hand and they spoke earnestly to each other in French for a couple of minutes, Tom's frustration at not being able to understand them growing by the second.

'*Au revoir*,' said Monsieur Petit, turning to Tom. '*Au revoir*, Josiah.'

'I'll see you out,' said Dr Harker, and the two men left and descended the stairs.

Tom crept to the stairwell and peered down.

At the bottom, instead of making for the front door, they turned towards the back of the house. Tom went to the window to see the stranger leaving by the back courtyard. As he lifted the latch of the door in the courtyard wall, the stranger turned and looked up. Tom leaped sideways out of view. Had he been seen? He was not sure.

Tom could hear Dr Harker's footsteps as he began to climb the stairs and he retreated back into the study. When the doctor entered, Tom was doing a very good job of looking fascinated by a book of geometry.

'Sorry about that, Tom,' said Dr Harker, taking off his wig and scratching at his scalp. 'Ah – that's better. Haven't seen Petit there for years.'

'Really?' said Tom, trying to sound uninterested. 'Have you known him for long, then?'

'Oh yes. For many years.'

'How do you know him?' Tom asked.

'How?' said Dr Harker, looking a little flustered. 'I don't know, Tom. I . . . erm . . . You know how it is, Tom.'

Tom had no idea how it was, but said nothing.

'But enough of Monsieur Petit!' The doctor

slapped his hand down on a pile of books. 'It is your birthday tomorrow, is it not? Your sixteenth birthday?'

'Well, yes it is, Dr Harker,' said Tom.

'Then we must mark it in some way, don't you think? Of course we must! What do you say, Tom? What shall we do?'

'Well, sir, I should love to go to the theatre. My father never wanted to go and—'

'Excellent!' said Dr Harker. 'The theatre it shall be! We'll have a marvellous time.'

'Thank you, Dr Harker,' said Tom. 'But what shall we see?'

'Well, I really think that ought to be for you to decide. What will it be, Tom? Shakespeare? Johnson?'

'I rather thought that I might like to see . . .' began Tom.

'Yes?' said Dr Harker with a smile.

'Well, I rather thought I might like to see an opera, Dr Harker.'

The doctor's face fell. 'An opera, you say?'

'Yes,' said Tom. 'But if you would rather . . .'

'No, no,' said Dr Harker, regaining his good

cheer. 'If you want to see an opera, then an opera you shall see.'

Tom grinned.

'Excellent,' the doctor added, a little hesitantly. 'Excellent . . .'

Tom and Dr Harker were soon hard at work on the doctor's collection. Shelf by shelf, drawer by drawer, item after item would be taken out and dusted down and given a label with its own number. Tom would ask Dr Harker what the item was called and would then make an entry in his best script in a huge leather-bound ledger on the doctor's desk.

Of course, this process was not a swift one, as every time Tom asked what an item was, it would trigger a lecture about its history and the people who made it and a lengthy reminiscence about the adventure connected with collecting it. Neither Tom nor the doctor in any way minded this, though; for Tom it was an education and for Dr Harker it was a chance to relive the excitement of his youth and give vent to his enthusiasm for his treasures.

Tom dreamed of travelling, and Dr Harker's

tales of his own travels fed his dreams. Normally, Tom would listen intently to every word the doctor said, sailing away with him in his imagination, paddling canoes along twisting rivers, riding horses across wide open plains, but today he found himself letting the words drift away into the background while the voice of the stranger he had met earlier grew in volume.

For Monsieur Petit might have been speaking French when he left, but he was speaking English when Tom arrived at the study door, he was sure of that. And more – much more strange than that, he had been speaking with a very particular accent: a *Scottish* accent.

ABOUT THE AUTHOR

Chris Priestley was born in Hull, spent his childhood in Wales and Gibraltar and his teens in Newcastle upon Tyne. He went to art college in Manchester and then lived and worked in London for many years as an illustrator and cartoonist, mainly for newspapers and magazines. He has written a range of books for children, both fiction and non-fiction. He lives in Norfolk with his wife and son.

The Tom Marlowe Adventures are inspired by his own childhood love of historical novels. *Death and the Arrow* was shortlisted for an Edgar Award by the Mystery Writers of America in 2004 and *Redwulf's Curse* was shortlisted for the 2006 Lancashire Fantastic Book Award.

Redwulf's Curse

BY CHRIS PRIESTLEY

The bones of Redwulf, an ancient warrior
king, lie in barren marshland. Anyone who
disturbs them will be cursed . . .

When Tom Marlowe and his wise friend, Dr
Harker, visit Norfolk they are intrigued by stories of
the ancient royal grave protected by a ghostly
guardian. As the wind whispers across the marshy
landscape, strange rumours are heard, mysterious
attacks are perpetrated and horrible deaths occur.
When Tom glimpses a mournful figure on the
horizon he cannot help wondering if there is any
truth to the legend. Surrounded by shifty-looking
servants, smugglers and a black-cloaked aristocrat,
anything seems possible to Tom. Can he tell legend
from fact, truth from lies and solve this mystery?

The third Tom Marlowe Adventure
978 0 552 55483 1

VICTORY

Susan Cooper

Two lives. Two struggles. One battle . . .

Sam Robbins is a farm boy, kidnapped and forced to serve aboard HMS Victory. Lord Nelson's ship at the Battle of Trafalgar in 1805. At first Sam is terrified and seasick, but in the rowdy, dangerous world of the warship, he transforms himself into a sailor and survives a fearsome and bloody battle, the echoes of which reach through the years to touch Molly Jennings. She is a modern-day English girl forced to leave London and live with her new step-family in America, and she too is fighting a battle against loss and loneliness.

This extraordinary time-shifting adventure tells the interwoven stories of Sam and Molly, linked by a mystery. Two lives joined forever by the touch of Nelson, one of the greatest sailors of all time.

978 0 370 32891 1

WOLF GIRL

Theresa Tomlinson

*How far would you go to save your mother
from the hangman's rope?*

Cwen, a poor weaver struggling to make a living
at Whitby Abbey, is accused of possessing a
valuable necklace. If found guilty she could
be hanged, burned or stoned. Wulfram, Cwen's
daughter, desperate to prove her mother's
innocence, encounters lies and treachery
wherever she turns for help.

Set in a turbulent period of Anglo-Saxon
England, this is a story of a resourceful,
dauntless heroine, determined and clever as
a wolf. Defying rank and convention, braving
wind, weather and marauding armies, Wulfran
shows that courage has its own just reward.

978 0 552 55271 4